"Oh, here's my gra— already," Mrs. Turn— said. "Come in, Daniel, and meet the new schoolteacher, Marie Bolden."

He was more handsome than she'd noticed at the rodeo. His reddish-brown hair had a tendency to curl. His eyes were clear and steady, and he towered over her by several inches, so she knew he must be six feet tall or more, with shoulders that were firm and well-balanced. No wonder he had captured her attention when she'd observed him riding a bucking bronco at the fair in Canaan. His was a striking face, framed by thick hair, with the cheekbones finely cut, a thin, slightly Roman nose, a firm chin and intensely blue eyes.

When she'd accepted this job in Cades Cove, she knew that meeting him was inevitable. She had dreaded the meeting, but had also looked forward to seeing him again. This first meeting hadn't been a disappointment.

He shook her hand, saying, "Most of the schoolmarms we've had in the Cove have been men or middle-aged women. It's high time the school authorities hired a woman who's easy on the eyes. Welcome to Cades Cove, Miss Bolden."

IRENE BRAND

has been publishing inspirational fiction since 1984. She has already published, or is under contract for, fifty titles of inspirational romances. She's had two novellas published, as well as three nonfiction books.

She's been a member of RWA since 1986. Irene was a public school teacher for twenty-three years until she retired in 1989 to devote full time to writing. She's received the Excellence in Inspirational Romance Writing Award, 1986, Blue Ridge Christian Writers Conference, the Koala Award for Quality Christian Writing, CWFI, 1991, the JUG (Just Uncommonly Good Writing) Award, West Virginia Writers, 1999, the First Runner-Up in the category of ARTS, West Virginia Women's Commission, 2001 and the First-Place Award, 2001 Celebrate Women Award, given by the General Federation of Women's Clubs, West Virginia.

Irene is active in her local church, serving currently as an adult Sunday school teacher, choir director and pianist. A native West Virginian, Irene holds an AB degree in secondary education and a master's degree in history from Marshall University. She's married to Rod Brand (no children), and their travels include thirty-five foreign countries and all fifty states of the United States.

IRENE BRAND

A Love

to

Treasure

HEARTSONG
PRESENTS

Recycling programs for this product may not exist in your area.

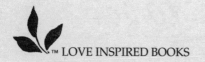

™ LOVE INSPIRED BOOKS

ISBN-13: 978-0-373-48664-9

A LOVE TO TREASURE

Copyright © 2013 by Irene Brand

www.LoveInspiredBooks.com

Printed in U.S.A.

But let all those that put their trust in thee rejoice;
let them ever shout for joy, because thou defendest
them: let them also that love thy name be joyful in thee.
—*Psalms* 5:11

To my niece, Catherine Yauger, who is more like a sister, and to her nephew, David Yauger

Chapter 1

August 1899

For the first time in her life, Marie Bolden was disregarding her father's wishes. Despite the fact that Vance Bolden was her stepfather, there had always been a close bond between the two of them. In fact, she felt as close to Vance as she did her biological mother, Evelyn. So when Vance said, "Marie, I *do not* want you to take that teaching job in Cades Cove," Marie was miserable when she had to answer, "But I can't go back on my word now. I've already signed the contract."

"Which you shouldn't have done without discussing it with your mother and me," he retorted.

Marie held to her decision. "If you didn't want

me to teach school, why did you send me to college in Columbia?"

"As you well know, I didn't approve of that, either, but you and your mother ganged up on me, and I finally agreed. Regardless, I thought when you finished school, you'd come home, marry one of the fine young men in this area and produce some grandchildren for Evelyn and me to enjoy in our old age."

Feeling terrible that she and her father were arguing, but determined to pursue her calling, Marie continued, "Did you think I would spend those two years of hard study at the women's seminary learning to teach and not put my knowledge to practical use?"

Vance shook his head angrily. "I expected you to graduate with honors, as you did, then marry a good man and start raising a family. I'd like to have some grandchildren before I get too old to enjoy them. Obviously, your brother doesn't intend to marry."

"Oh, don't give up on Earl yet. Just because he's been living in the mountains with the Cherokee doesn't mean that he'll never marry. He just wants to live the life of a hermit for a few years." Earl had gone to the mountains upon returning from fighting in Cuba, where he'd contracted malaria. With their various herbs, the medicine men had cured him. "I think he's already learned that living alone in a log cabin isn't very pleasant. At least the last time I saw him, he indicated that he'll probably get married someday—when the right woman comes along."

"I hope so," Vance said, "as long as he doesn't marry a Cherokee. I want him to come home and take over our property here in Canaan when I get too old to manage it on my own."

Although Marie held her stepfather in high regard, as far as she was concerned, his bias against the Native Americans was a flaw in his character. Marie knew that this prejudice could be traced to the War Between the States, when the Cherokee nation had sided with the Union rather than the Confederacy. But that war had ended a long time ago. Still, when she considered the suffering Vance and other Southerners had endured during those years, she understood his sentiments, even if she didn't agree with them.

Grinning, she asked, "With all the trouble we've caused you, have you ever been sorry you rescued our mother?" Vance had found their pregnant mother afloat in the Atlantic, then later married her and adopted Marie and Earl as his own.

"Don't joke about a thing like that. You know how much I love your mother. I'll admit it was a marriage of convenience at first, but it didn't take long for me to realize she was the best thing that had ever happened to me. Besides, you can't doubt that I love you and Earl."

Marie put her arm around her father's waist and hugged him. "And we love you."

"Then will you give up this crazy idea of teaching school in Cades Cove? With all those bootleggers, renegade Cherokees and who knows who else living there, it's not safe for you to live in that area."

"I'm sorry to go against your wishes, Dad, but

I've agreed to teach in the Cove, and I'm going. You seem to think that I've accepted this teaching position just to irritate you. That isn't true. I believe that I can make a difference in the lives of the children. It's such an isolated place that many people avoid settling in the area, but I know the children who live there need an education. I feel it is my responsibility to work with them. Surely you would expect me to use my education."

"I expected you to teach here in Canaan, if you just had to teach."

"There isn't an opening for a teacher here," Marie said patiently, as if they hadn't had this conversation several other times. "I'm fortunate to find a place to teach anywhere, because many areas still prefer to have a male teacher. I feel that I've been called to teach, somewhat like Mother was called to be a missionary in this country."

"There are times when it pays to be a stepfather," Vance said peevishly. "At least you can't claim you got your stubbornness from me."

Laughing, Marie put her arms around his waist. "It's a good thing Mother didn't hear that comment, unless you think I inherited that trait from my biological father."

She paused a moment, thinking about the father she'd never seen, a man who had drowned before he could start his missionary work in the United States. According to her mother, Marie had inherited many of his physical characteristics—straight brown hair, clear and steady eyes, a firm mouth and a strong chin. The last time she'd seen her twin brother, Earl, they still bore a remarkable resemblance to one another, so she supposed she would readily recognize him if they met again after all this time.

"You know I love your mother devotedly, so don't try to change the subject," Vance said. "My objection is that Cades Cove is no place for a young unmarried woman to live. It has the reputation of being a wild area. Evelyn and I will be worried about you. It still isn't too late to change your mind."

"Oh, I'll get along fine." Patting him on the shoulder, she continued, "Remember I've had parents who taught me to be self-reliant. I haven't found a man yet that I want to marry, so I'm going to try teaching school for one season. If I'm a failure, then I may look around for a husband, but I suppose you'll want to investigate his background before you'll let me marry him."

Even without having him look into the background of Daniel Watson, she knew that neither of her parents would approve of a marriage to him.

"Very funny," Vance said. "But, if you're determined to have your way, I'm going to take you to Cades Cove, and if I don't consider it a good place for you, you'll have to come home."

Marie shook her head, stood on tiptoes and kissed him. "You know I've already given my word and I'm obligated to teach in the Cove. Besides, I'll be staying in the home of Lena Turner. She's the sister of our pastor's wife and has a good reputation. She'll advise me on what to do and what not to do."

"Just the same, I'm going with you to look over the situation. I'll take my saddle horse, too, and we'll take your horse and you can keep the buggy. If school teaching up there is like it is here, you'll probably be expected to visit the parents, and you'll need some transportation. I'll arrange with your landlady to pay for the keep of the horse."

Laughing, Marie started up the steps to her bedroom to finish packing. Now that the time had come to leave, she was reluctant to say goodbye to her parents. She sat down and looked out her bedroom window toward the village of Canaan, but her mind was elsewhere. She apparently *had* inherited the wanderlust of her parents, who had been shipwrecked along the Atlantic Coast near Charleston, South Carolina, in 1875, when her father had been drowned. Vance Bolden had rescued her mother, Evelyn, and had assisted her in giving birth to twins while a horrific storm blasted the coast.

Soon afterward, Vance had married Evelyn, taking her and her newborn babes on the long wagon journey from Charleston to the mountains of North Carolina. Sometimes she wondered what kind of life she would have had if Vance hadn't adopted them. Because he'd been such a good father, and because he had paid for her education, it was stressful to be making a move of which he didn't approve.

It was true that she felt a divine calling to teach in Cades Cove, but she was glad she'd experienced the urge to move there before she met Daniel Watson. After seeing him, she wondered if she had an ulterior motive in wanting to work in the Cove. What would her father say if he knew that a suspected bootlegger was one of the main reasons she was looking forward to teaching in an isolated area of the state?

Marie had never met a man who'd interested her romantically until she'd encountered Daniel. She hadn't even spoken to him, but after seeing him once, she couldn't get him out of her mind. Since she'd always kept rigid control over her emotions, it annoyed her that her thoughts had strayed to him often after she'd seen him for the first time riding a bucking bronco.

For years the town of Canaan had sponsored a rodeo to celebrate the Fourth of July, and hundreds of people attended the special event. Daniel had received the highest award by riding a bronco that was reputed to have killed a couple of riders in the past. The crowd had waited spellbound as the horse threw rider after rider and trampled on one man before he could reach the safety zone. Daniel was the last rider, and he'd actually seemed to enjoy the antics of the animal, which had bucked and cavorted all over the field trying to rid himself of the human who stuck to him like a leech. Rather than being thrown, Daniel had walked away with a trophy and a cash award, too, smiling and waving to the onlookers as though the masterful riding was all in a day's work.

She'd wondered who he was and asked a neighbor, Mary Tyler, who sat beside her. "Oh, that's Daniel Watson," Mary answered.

Marie decided that she must look puzzled, because Mary said, "Surely you've heard of him!"

"I don't think so. Remember, I've been attending school for a couple of years in South Carolina, and I don't know everyone now as I did when I was a child. Does Daniel live in this area?"

"Yes, as a boy he stayed with his grandmother, Lena Turner, who lives in Cades Cove, northwest of here. Daniel inherited a farm there after he returned from the Spanish-American War." The woman leaned close to Marie and whispered, "I understand he makes and sells moonshine. That's the way a lot of families in the Cove make their living, or so I've heard."

"Oh!" Marie said in dismay. "I'm going to board with Mrs. Turner when I start teaching in Cades Cove. She was recommended highly by one of Mother's friends who has relatives living in the area. I didn't doubt that it was a good place for me to board when I made arrangements to live with her. Now I'm not so sure."

"You have no reason to fret about it. Mrs. Turner is a fine woman," Mary said. "You couldn't find any better place to live. I'm sure she doesn't approve of what her grandson is doing."

Marie laughed softly. "I hope Father doesn't hear about her grandson's reputation, for he's already opposed to my teaching school in the Cove. Regardless, I'm not going to back out now. Apparently it isn't easy to find a teacher for the area. No doubt that's the reason the job was available."

"I didn't mean to give the area a bad reputation," Mary said. "Most of the people in the Cove are Christians and good law-abiding citizens, and there are several churches in that area. As far as that's concerned, Daniel Watson is well thought of. It's just hearsay that he owns a moonshine still, so it may not be true. Besides, many people don't think it's a crime to make liquor and distribute it. Not that I believe it's all right, because you know my family are teetotalers, but those folks consider it a crop to sell, like vegetables or grains of any kind."

"It's certainly a crime in our household, so I hope Father doesn't realize that there's any connection between my landlady and the Cove's bootlegger."

"It's my opinion that Cades Cove has gotten its tarnished reputation from a few hoodlums who get in trouble and go to a place called Chestnut Flats to hide from the authorities. For the most part, the people who live there are God-fearing, reputable citizens. Just go to the Cove with an open mind, and you'll get along fine."

After her talk with Mary, Marie climbed the small hill behind their brick home, where she had not only a good view of Canaan, but also of the hills beyond the village. Somehow she sensed that this move to Cades Cove was going to be the breaking point between her and the home she'd known all of her life. Of course, she'd be coming home often, but still, she was making a break with the past. She would no longer be Vance and Evelyn's "little" girl, for she was going out on her own, and it was a parting that touched her heart.

"God," she whispered, "I pray for Your guidance. I'm afraid of the future, and I'm sad to let go of the past. Should I have been satisfied to stay here in my parents' home until I became a married woman? I know I'll make mistakes, but grant me the guidance I need in this venture into the future."

The next morning, after kissing her mother goodbye, Marie sat beside her father in the buggy and, with anticipation and excitement, started off on the new venture. His riding horse was tied to the rear of the buggy, for he would return home on his horse and leave the buggy for Marie to ride back and forth to the school in Cades Cove. The offer of the teaching job had come so suddenly that she hadn't had the opportunity to learn much about the area where she'd be living. The man who was supposed to teach that year had supposedly found a better position and his resignation left a vacancy, so Marie had been offered the job. She'd only had a week's notice, and although she didn't want her parents to suspect it, she was somewhat apprehensive about taking the job.

"Tell me something about Cades Cove, Dad," she said. "What can I expect? I understand that I'll only have about fifteen or twenty students of all ages, so I packed only the books I thought I'd need to get started. Mother said you would bring supplies to me if I can't get away to visit you."

"Yes, I will. If you're determined to do this," he

said grumpily, "I want you to be the best teacher you possibly can be. It's said that there are about a hundred people living in the Cove, although some of them are transients. They just stay for a month or two, then travel on westward to greener pastures."

"Mrs. Turner doesn't have any children in the school, but she's interested in the education of the young people in the area. She's the former schoolteacher, but she's in her seventies and decided the students needed some 'new blood,' as she said when she visited us in town. I just hope I turn out to be a good teacher."

"Of course you're going to be a good teacher," Vance said.

Laughing, she said, "You know, you might be prejudiced on that subject. What else do you know about the Cove?"

"The history of the Cove goes back a long ways. As early as the 1700s the Cherokee used two main trails to cross the Smoky Mountains from North Carolina to Tennessee. One of the trails passed through there. By the latter part of the eighteenth century, the Cherokee had established a settlement in Cades Cove, known then as the Otter Place."

"Does that mean there were otters in the region?"

Shrugging his shoulders and slapping the horse gently with the end of the reins, Vance said, "That's generally thought to be true, but there weren't any otters in the cove when the first European settlers arrived. It was an isolated region, and we don't know much about what the area was like."

Marie listened eagerly as her father talked of the history of the Cove, always looking westward, where she could see high, rugged mountains in the distance.

"I know that living conditions won't be as comfortable as in Canaan, but I'm not expecting luxury. Although the population is sparse," she added, "the Cove isn't cut off from the rest of the world. It even has phone service now, although it's not too reliable according to people who try to communicate with that area. Still, I can probably call and talk to you and Mother occasionally."

Another hour's drive brought them to the entrance of Cades Cove, and Vance paused when he saw a man sitting on the porch of an unpainted one-story frame dwelling. The man, with a full face of white whiskers, was dressed in a cotton shirt rolled to his elbows and a pair of faded overalls. A woman stood in the doorway. She was barefooted and wore a black cotton skirt that came to her ankles, and a white long-sleeved blouse. Her black hair was parted in the middle and pulled into a tight bun on the back of her neck. Two untidy children, a boy and a girl, clung to her skirt and peeped around their mother. The girl was sucking her thumb, and Marie's optimistic view of her students suffered a setback. She took a deep breath. If this family was typical of the students she would teach, it would be a difficult experience, although she hadn't expected her task to be an easy one.

Speaking to the man, Vance said, "We're looking for the home of Lena Turner. Can you give us directions?"

The man spat a mouthful of tobacco juice on the ground before he answered. "Go on down this road for a piece. You'll find Mrs. Turner livin' in the second building on yore right."

Thanking him, Vance moved on, and Marie decided that her face must have mirrored the trepidation she was experiencing, for her father said quietly, "I doubt that family is typical of what most of the residents are like. There are many prosperous and educated people in the Cove. Still, you may have many students who are behind others their age in both learning and social skills. No doubt it will be a challenge."

Grinning and spreading her hands wide in resignation, Marie said, "I'll be all right. I didn't expect to find towns like Charleston, Asheville or even Canaan in these mountains."

She was, however, relieved when they reached Mrs. Turner's house to see a two-story frame house in excellent repair, with blooming flowers lining the walkway. A slender gray-haired woman, dressed neatly in an ankle-length, brown cotton skirt and long-sleeve white blouse, rose from a rocking chair on the porch and hurried down the walk to greet them.

"I'm Lena Turner, and I'm glad you could come to teach our children. Welcome!"

Vance took Marie's hand to help her step from the buggy, and by the time he had secured the horse and buggy to a convenient hitching post, Mrs. Turner had reached them.

"My!" Mrs. Turner said, with a welcoming smile on her face. "I'm so happy to see you. You're much younger and prettier than I remembered. We've got lots of bachelors in this area who will be happy to see you, too. Or have you already got a special fellow?"

Not yet able to get a word in edgewise, Marie shook her head.

"Regardless, welcome to Cades Cove and to my home. I taught the school for several years, so I'm pleased to board the schoolteacher. I live alone, and I've got an extra bedroom. Besides, I enjoy company."

Encouraged by the woman's smile and her kind welcome, Marie's spirits lifted.

"Thank you," she said, shaking Mrs. Turner's outstretched hand. Believing that she *was* really welcome, she turned to Vance.

"This is my father, Vance Bolden," Marie said, pride evident in her voice.

"Come in! Come in!" Mrs. Turner said. "I have some cold tea and freshly baked cookies for you."

"I intend to return to Canaan before nightfall, so I can't stay long," Vance said, "but I am thirsty. Should I bring Marie's suitcases in now?"

"Yes, of course. But I also have a full meal prepared, so we will eat before you start on your way. How far is it to Canaan?"

"We've been on the road five hours," Vance said,

"but some of that was climbing mountains. My return trip probably won't take as long."

He carried Marie's possessions and placed them in the bedroom Mrs. Turner indicated. Marie noticed his sigh of relief to learn that she would have such a pleasant place to stay.

Showing them to the washroom, Mrs. Turner said, "You can freshen up while I put food on the table."

When Marie returned to the living room, the food was ready. Vance soon appeared, and Mrs. Turner invited them into the dining room. By the time they'd eaten heartily of the meal of chicken, dumplings, green beans and apple pie, Marie felt right at home in the Turner household. She could tell by her father's expression that he was also pleased with the arrangements, content that she would be in a safe environment.

Although she'd gotten accustomed to being away from home during the two years she'd attended school in Charleston, Marie couldn't help feeling a little forlorn when Vance left shortly after they'd eaten. She considered her father as strong and reliant as the Rock of Gibraltar, and she already felt despondent to be separated from him and her mother. Reminding herself that it had been her decision to leave home, she followed Vance out to the road, and he kissed her on both cheeks before climbing onto his horse. She noticed the tears glistening in his eyes—the first time she'd ever known her father to cry—and she prayed that she wouldn't start crying, too.

"Remember," he said, "if things don't work out for

you here in the Cove and you want to come home, we'll be glad to see you."

"I'll remember," she said, and stood by the fence watching him ride away.

Mrs. Turner waited on the porch, and perhaps noticing Marie's sorrow, she said sympathetically, "You have a fine father."

Sniffing childishly, Marie said, "I know. I've been blessed with both my mother and father. I'm going to miss them, but I can't stay at home forever."

As they started into the house, Marie heard a horse cantering down the road. She turned, just as Daniel Watson swung out of the saddle and tied his mount to the hitching rail in front of the house. She was momentarily breathless, for she'd been hoping she wouldn't see him so soon, if at all. She'd thought of him too often after she saw him for the first time.

"Oh, here's my grandson to meet you already," Mrs. Turner said. "Come in, Daniel, and meet the new schoolteacher, Marie Bolden."

He dismounted and hugged his grandmother, which brought a smile to her face. Mrs. Turner was obviously proud of her handsome grandson, and Marie could understand why.

Seeing him face-to-face, she realized that he was more good-looking than she'd noticed at the rodeo. His reddish-brown hair had a tendency to curl. His eyes were clear and steady, and he towered over her by several inches, so she knew he must be six feet tall or more, with a set of shoulders that were firm and well-balanced. No wonder he had captured her attention when she'd observed him riding a bucking bronco at the fair in Canaan. His was a striking face, framed by thick hair, with finely cut cheekbones, a thin, slightly Roman nose, a firm chin and intensely blue eyes.

When she'd accepted this job in Cades Cove, she knew that meeting him was inevitable. She had dreaded the meeting, but had also looked forward to seeing him again. This first meeting hadn't been a disappointment.

He shook her hand, saying, "Most of the school-marms we've had in the Cove have been men or middle-aged women. It's high time the school authorities hired a woman who's easy on the eyes. Welcome to Cades Cove, Miss Bolden."

Although deep in her heart, she had relished the thought that she would see Daniel more often in Cades Cove than if she remained in Canaan, she hadn't expected to meet him the first few hours after she'd arrived. This sudden meeting had caused her to be somewhat breathless, and she felt light-headed. If meeting Daniel for the first time had such an effect on her, she wondered if she'd made a mistake in coming to Cades Cove.

Chapter 2

To Marie's relief, Daniel didn't tarry long, and she welcomed the privacy of her room to deal with her emotions. When she had attended school in Charleston, she'd met several young gentlemen whose company she'd enjoyed, but none of them had made any lasting impression on her. The thing that distressed her more than any other was the possibility that this infatuation with Daniel would interfere with her effectiveness as a teacher. Marie wished with all her heart that she could discuss the situation with her mother, but knowing that was impossible, she resorted to prayer.

Kneeling beside the bed, she buried her face in the soft feather mattress.

"God," she whispered, "what am I going to do?

Since I was a little girl, I've dreamed of finding the right man for a husband, but I wanted him to be someone like my papa." After seeing Daniel two times, she definitely knew that he wasn't another Vance Bolden.

Marie took off her shoes and lay on the soft bed without removing her clothes. It seemed that every nerve in her body was on edge, but when she was awakened by Mrs. Turner's soft knock, she was surprised that she'd gone to sleep.

"Yes?" she said.

"I'm just checking to see if you want to go see the schoolhouse today or wait until tomorrow," Mrs. Turner said.

"How far away is it?"

"About a mile and a half."

Considering that the school might not be in good condition and therefore be a big disappointment to her, Marie said, "I'm really curious about the school, and I want to see it as soon as possible, but I believe it might be best for me to wait until morning."

"That will be fine. I asked Daniel to stable your horse and put the buggy in the barn so it will be out of the weather if we should have a thunderstorm."

"Thanks very much. I'm going to unpack my clothes now."

"Let me know if I can be of any help."

As Daniel left his grandmother's home and headed toward his farm in the northern section of the Cove, he was annoyed about something. Usually when he visited her, he came away with a feeling that all was right with the world. What was the problem? When he arrived at his farm and stabled his horse, he walked toward his two-story frame house and sprawled out in a rocker on the porch.

During his months in the army, he'd observed that many of his fellow soldiers, during the months of training before they sailed for Cuba, had married. Seemingly they needed the fellowship of women, and although he enjoyed the company of the women he'd met, he'd never met any woman that had made an impression on him as Marie Bolden had made. He didn't like it. Daniel had never considered taking a wife, but now he wondered if he'd been wrong. Was it possible that after seeing a woman only once he could have a serious affection for her?

"Well, that's not going to be the case in this situation," Daniel mumbled. "I'm satisfied with my life just as it is, and I don't intend to let Marie Bolden or any other woman change that!"

When Marie awakened the next morning, the house seemed quiet, and she surmised that Mrs. Turner hadn't gotten up yet. Tired after the buggy ride and the frustration of sleeping in a different bed, Marie was glad that she'd rested most of the night. Hoping that she could have the day free of distractions to become oriented to the job she'd undertaken, Marie anticipated visiting the schoolhouse to get an idea of the preparations she needed to make before school started.

But a day free of distractions was not to be. Daniel came in the kitchen door while Marie and his grandmother were still eating their breakfast. Lena insisted on frying eggs and bacon for him, but when he convinced her that he'd already eaten, she poured a cup of coffee for him, and he sat down and drank that while they finished eating.

"I came by to see if you need any help taking your things to the schoolhouse," he said to Marie.

Although she had seen Daniel only once before their first meeting, and hadn't spoken to him then, she'd gotten the idea that Daniel was self-centered. Thus his offer surprised her so much she accepted his help without considering that she had already decided it might not be wise to spend much time in this man's company.

On the other hand, was she judging him on hearsay rather than on anything she'd personally detected in his actions? After she'd seen him at the rodeo, she'd discreetly questioned Mrs. Turner's sister, Pearl, who had nothing but kind remarks about Daniel.

She told Pearl, "I don't like to admit that my father is right, but I'm wondering if I might be making a mistake by walking into a situation that will cause me a lot of trouble. I don't expect to have a carefree school year, but I don't want to be involved in a feud of some kind either."

"If I were you," Pearl said, "I would go to Cades Cove with an open mind. Don't borrow trouble."

Acting on that advice, she'd pushed worry aside and looked forward to this new experience.

Now she said to Daniel, "I appreciate your offer, for I will need some help. I have two boxes of books, which are quite heavy. I didn't want to bring a lot of supplies until I looked over the situation. I still have some boxes packed at home, and Father will bring them to me when I want them. I thought it was better to see how well equipped the school is before I brought things from home. If I need anything, I'll contact Father."

"I go to Canaan occasionally, too," Daniel said, "so if you want me to bring anything, let me know. I'll check with you when I make a trip down that way."

Marie nodded her thanks and acceptance of his offer, before she said, "One thing I haven't learned is how many students I'll have and what age groups."

Daniel looked at his grandmother. "Do you know, Granny?"

"It's hard to say," Lena stated. "Some of the parents may refuse to send their children, and there isn't any law saying they have to. Also, a few children living in Chestnut Flats don't attend school, but that area doesn't have a good reputation, so most teachers haven't bothered to insist that the children come to school. To give the parents their due, they believe they can teach their kids as much as they need to know at home, which they can't, of course."

"I can't imagine why parents would refuse to send their children to school," Marie said.

"When parents don't have an education them-selves, they can't understand why it's important," Lena said. "Children are needed to work in the fields when they're very young, and they don't know any other life."

Laughing, Daniel said, "And Granny is too nice to tell you that some parents won't trust you to teach their children because you're a woman."

Frowning, Marie said, "I know. I've been warned by my parents, my friends, my neighbors and even my professors at college. 'A woman's place is in the home' are words I've heard so much that I feel as if they've been seared into my brain with a hot iron."

Daniel laughed again, and Lena said, "Stop it, Daniel. It isn't funny!"

"Oh, let him alone," Marie said with a slight smile. "I'm used to the prejudice by now."

"I'm sorry," Daniel apologized. "I don't have anything against female teachers. I was amused at the disgusted expression on your face. It was fierce enough to make a mummy laugh."

"Well, you're not a mummy, so behave yourself," Lena said.

Daniel's presence unsettled Marie, so she excused herself, went to her room and tried to determine what had happened to her when she had met him. She'd never before experienced the speeding of her heart-beat when she met any man for the first time. When she'd been in college, several of the men who at-tended the nearby seminary had evinced consid-erable interest in her. Remembering her manners,

Marie hadn't rebuffed them as she'd wanted to do, but had treated them pleasantly without giving them even a slight hint that she was interested in them as possible suitors. It would be unheard of for a married woman to be teaching school, and she hadn't yet met a man who was more important to her than her teaching career. Had that changed when she met Daniel Watson?

When Marie came back downstairs, she tried to speak normally as she said to Lena, "I don't mind admitting that I'm a nervous wreck, wondering if I have the knowledge to start teaching, but I've already made the decision. I won't quit now. I don't like to impose on you," Marie said to Lena, "but perhaps you could find time to ride with me through the Cove, and show me where the students live."

"Certainly I'll go with you. Anytime."

When the breakfast dishes were done and Marie had packed a small lunch for herself, Daniel said, "If you'll show me where those boxes are that you want hauled to the schoolhouse, I'll load them in the buggy for you."

"That would be helpful," Mrs. Turner said. "I was going with Marie to show her where the schoolhouse is located, but I wouldn't be very helpful unloading boxes. Do you have time to carry her supplies into the schoolhouse, too?"

When Daniel assured her that he had some spare time, Mrs. Turner said, "Her horse and buggy are in the barn, so please bring them around to the front of the house."

"Oh, I don't want to put you to that bother," Marie protested. "I know how to harness a horse, and I'm sure I can find the school."

"It isn't any bother to show you the way. I intended to cut hay today, but that hard rain we had earlier in the week flattened it. I'm going to wait a day or two to see if it will straighten up before I try to stack it."

"Really, it isn't necessary," Marie insisted again, determined that she wouldn't get involved with this man. "If you point me in the right direction, I'm sure I won't miss the schoolhouse. I understand that there's only one school in the Cove."

"Only one," Daniel said, "but considering we have less than a hundred residents here, so far we haven't needed more than one school. Not only will I load the books for you, I'll go with you and take them into the building. It's about two miles to the schoolhouse. I'll tether my horse to the buggy so I can leave from there. You can find your own way home, I'm sure."

Marie got the impression that Daniel was a person who wouldn't take no for an answer, and knowing it would be helpful for him to carry her books and teaching supplies into the school, she didn't press the point. However, if Daniel Watson thought she would take orders from him, he was mistaken. Albert Sinclair, a school trustee, was the one who'd contacted her about the job, and he was the one she'd depend on for assistance and advice.

Daniel carried the books from the house, placed them in the back of her buggy and rode beside her as they went to the schoolhouse. Although she had sized Daniel up as being egotistical, she was surprised that he encouraged her to talk about herself. By the time they reached the school, she didn't know any more about him than she had when they were first introduced, but he had learned quite a lot about her.

"So why did you choose to become a teacher?" he asked.

"My parents wanted both my twin brother and me to go to college, but Earl absolutely refused to go. I didn't particularly relish the idea of leaving home for that long, either, but I didn't want to disappoint them, too."

"You have a brother by the name of Earl?" he said, seemingly surprised.

"Yes, Earl Bolden. He lives in this area someplace, but he doesn't keep in touch with the family. He's only returned to Canaan a few times since he left home. Do you know him?"

"Well, I'm not sure," Daniel said slowly. "There's a hermit by the name of Earl living up in the mountains. He comes to Cades Cove once or twice a year for food supplies and ammunition. Mostly, however, he lives off the land."

Laughing, Marie said, "That's Earl, all right. Whatever possesses him to live like that, none of us know. I suppose there's a streak of wanderlust in our family. My father and mother left England before we were born to become missionaries in this country. They intended to live among the Cherokee and minister to them, but they were involved in a shipwreck not far from the South Carolina coast. My father drowned, but Vance Bolden rescued my mother, and we were born a day or so later, which ended their missionary plans for the time being. Vance took all of us to his plantation and, before he moved to this area, he asked my mother to marry him. I've heard people refer to marriages like theirs as a 'marriage of convenience.' I suppose it was, to some extent, but they're still happily married after all these years."

Daniel looked at her intently. "I've only seen Earl a few times, but I think that he resembles you. It's a small world," he added.

They turned a slight curve and the view before them was breathtaking. "Oh, my!" Marie said, struck dumb by the beauty of the scene. They had come to the head of a hollow. The valley had given way to a heavily forested area in the background. The oval area had two buildings—a white church with a soaring steeple—and a schoolhouse with a bell tower on it. Miles away in the background was a splendid view of the Smoky Mountains.

Marie sensed that Daniel was watching her, and he halted the horses.

"I've never seen a more beautiful sight," she murmured.

"I agree," he said quietly. "I didn't appreciate my home until I left it for about six months to fight in the Spanish-American War. That's all the traveling I wanted. I haven't strayed far from this area since I returned home."

Daniel lifted the reins and the horse moved forward. He stopped in front of the schoolhouse, but he pointed to the church across the road. "There are five churches in Cades Cove," he said, as he dismounted. "That one is the Baptist church where Granny attends."

During the short ride, Marie had decided that Daniel Watson wasn't nearly as bad as she'd thought on their first meeting, so she stifled her inclination to ask him if he went to church. Knowing she could learn that information from Lena, instead she said, "Well, I guess I'd better take a look at the interior of the schoolhouse. I don't know what to expect."

He circled the buggy and reached up to help her step down. "I don't remember that I've ever been in another schoolhouse, so I'm not a good judge, however, I consider it a well-constructed building. It isn't as old as the church. The original school burned a few years ago. Some people think the fire wasn't an accident but was arson by a disgruntled group of men from Chestnut Flats."

Taking a key from his pocket, Daniel climbed the steps first and opened the door. "Wait on the steps," he suggested, "until I can get some light in here."

Marie's first impression of the interior of the large room was positive, and she sighed deeply. The area was hot and it smelled musty, but it probably hadn't been aired for several weeks. However, as Daniel moved from window to window raising the blinds and opening the outside shutters, she noticed that the furnishings of the room were adequate, maps hung on the walls and a bookcase held a large number of books. By the time she added the pictures she'd brought, several boxes of books and a large Bible, the room would look like a school. Her fingers tingled with anticipation to start teaching.

Daniel pointed to one desk. "That's where I sat the last three years I was in school. One day I carved my initials on the underside of the seat and thought the teacher wouldn't notice. He noticed, all right, and paddled me until I couldn't sit down for a week without a cushion under me. To add insult to injury, he made me sit in the same seat the next school year. I'd grown six inches by then and weighed about ten pounds more. I was miserable most of the year."

"Served you right," she said mischievously.

"I can see I won't get any sympathy from you," he said grumpily, but the mirth gleaming from his eyes took the sting out of his words.

Marie had experienced a few nightmares about what condition the school might be in, but she was well pleased with the structure and the interior of the building. After they unloaded all of the books and placed them on the shelves and stored her teaching supplies in a large, locked walk-in closet, she felt right at home.

When they started to leave the building, Daniel handed her the key. "It's all yours, but don't hesitate to let me know if I can be of any help."

"Thank you," she said, and added gratefully, "I wouldn't be halfway finished if you hadn't helped me, but I want to rest now."

Looking at her dirty hands, and the dust and

grime on her dress, she said, "I'm going back to your grandmother's home and wash off some of this dirt. She said something about roast beef and mashed potatoes for supper, and I don't want to miss that."

"Granny loves to cook, so I'm happy she decided to have you board at her house. I was somewhat distressed, thinking it might be too much for her, but after watching you work this morning, I'm sure you won't cause her any trouble."

Pleased at his praise, she said, "I've been falsely accused occasionally by people who say I'm the daughter of a rich man and don't have to work. It's true that my parents are well-off financially, but my mother insisted that I learn to be self-sufficient if the need to support myself should ever arise. My mother taught me to work around the house when I was growing up, and I learned to take care of myself when I was in school at Charleston. I didn't mind, for I wasn't content to sponge off my parents. I wanted to prove to myself, if not to others, that I'm not a spoiled brat. I figure your granny and I will be good for each other because I'll miss my parents, and she will fill that gap."

"We have phone service off and on here in the Cove, and Granny can usually reach me by phone. Have her try to call me if anything comes up that requires my help. I'll plan to come in my buggy in a few days, and we can drive around Cades Cove so you can see where your students live. Parents usually expect a visit from the new teacher. I'll probably check on you a few times until you get oriented."

"Thank you. I appreciate that," Marie said, and she meant it. In spite of her first impression of Daniel, she'd been content with his attitude today. Instead of telling her *what* to do as she'd expected him to, he waited for her to give him directions about moving the furniture and storing the books and school supplies she'd brought from home.

Daniel untied his horse from the back of the buggy and climbed gracefully into the saddle.

Marie sat down on the schoolhouse steps to eat her lunch. She waved goodbye to Daniel as he flipped the reins, and the horse trotted away. She had some time before she needed to return to Lena's for supper, so she decided to get to know the area where she'd be spending her days.

The nearby church building was surrounded by a cemetery with many headstones. When she wasn't so tired, she would spend some time wandering around the cemetery, but that would have to wait for another day.

Two men were cutting weeds in the cemetery, and she recognized one of them as Albert Sinclair, the man who'd interviewed her for the teaching job. Mr. Sinclair must have seen her at the same time she noticed him, for he raised his hand in greeting and walked toward her. She stood and shook hands with him.

"Did you find everything you need for the opening of school?" he asked.

"More than enough," Marie said. "Not knowing how well stocked your school would be, I brought several crates of school supplies, as well as books, so we shouldn't need to buy anything else for several months."

"Good! Good!" Sinclair said. "We try to supply the best for our pupils and teachers."

"Well, you certainly have. I pray that I won't disappoint you and the parents."

"I'm not expecting any problems along that line. The people I talked to in Canaan recommended you highly."

"I'll try my best to be the teacher this school needs, and if I should get out of line, please don't hesitate to tell me."

"I'll do that, of course, but the trustees will support you. If you have any problems, don't try to solve them on your own. Lena Turner is one of the trustees, as well as two of us men. Since you're living with her, you won't have to search far to get any help you need."

When Marie drove the buggy back to Lena's home, the landlady was sitting in her favorite rocking chair, crocheting, while visiting with a beautiful, fair-haired woman. The newcomer was dressed in a dark blue dress, which added to her lovely countenance. Groaning inwardly and comparing her appearance to the visitor's, Marie knew that she looked like a tramp. The pump on the well at the schoolhouse needed repairing and there hadn't been any water, so she couldn't wash her hands after they'd finished unpacking the school supplies. Wishing she had sneaked in the back door after she'd stabled her horse, Marie recalled the advice her mother had taught her from childhood. "Remember you're *my* daughter, and no matter what problems you encounter, I'm expecting you to hold up your head and say to yourself, 'I'm Vance and Evelyn Bolden's daughter, and I'm as good as anyone else.'"

Remembering this amused Marie, so despite the fact that her hands were filthy and her dress was wrinkled and dirty, she felt as if her mother was peering over her shoulder. Every bone in her body seemed to be aching, too, but she forced a smile and walked toward the porch.

Mentally, she said, "All right, Ma," the way she addressed her mother when she wanted to annoy her. "I'm a Bolden, and I never have to apologize for the way I look."

Still when she'd climbed the steps, she said, "Excuse my appearance. We don't have any water at the school yet, and I've been rearranging the room. It's pretty dusty."

"Doesn't matter," Lena said. "Sit down and rest a spell. I want you to meet our friend and neighbor, Viola Butler." Turning to her visitor, she introduced her, "This is our new schoolmarm, Marie Bolden."

Marie didn't want to sit down, but she did lean against a porch post to take the weight off her feet.

"Glad to meet you, Miss Bolden," Viola said. "Good luck with your teaching. Our teachers don't stay long—it's too isolated for them. And I don't blame them. I wish my parents would move someplace else—like Charleston. I feel as if I'm wasting my life in Cades Cove. The only way I'll ever get away is to marry someone who lives elsewhere, but I was foolish enough to fall in love with Daniel Watson, who thinks there's no place on earth that's comparable to Cades Cove."

Marie glanced toward Lena to see how she would react to this comment, but her landlady continued with her needlework, and Marie couldn't see her eyes.

"I can't imagine why a young, good-looking woman like you," Viola continued, "would want to bury herself in Cades Cove for nine months of the year."

Knowing that she'd already taken a dislike to Viola, Marie chose her words carefully.

"Actually I was delighted to have the opportunity. When I persuaded my parents to send me to college, they warned me that women schoolteachers aren't yet readily accepted by society. I had the same advice from my college professors, and I soon learned that was the true situation when I started applying for jobs."

"We're so pleased that you chose to come to our school," Lena said. "What with bootlegging, the reputation of Chestnut Flats and some parents who can't see the value of educating their children, especially daughters, there aren't many people willing to come to Cades Cove to teach. However, to balance the disadvantage, we do have numerous good citizens here, and many children who need to be pointed in the right direction. I prayed to God that we would find a dedicated teacher for the local school, and He answered that prayer by sending you to live among us."

Pleased with Lena's comment, Marie thanked her, then asked, "Where is Chestnut Flats? What's wrong with the people?"

At that moment she couldn't recall what she'd heard about the area, but she knew it wasn't complimentary.

"They're shiftless drunkards, and those of us on this side of the Cove don't have anything to do with them," Viola said.

"Speak for yourself, Viola," Lena commented tersely. "I have several close friends in Chestnut Flats. I'll never forget when my husband was dying, how kind the women were to spend hours sitting by his bedside giving me time to take care of my property, and also to check on Daniel's workers. That was a bleak six months—my husband dying and my grandson fighting in Cuba. I know that there are a few undesirable characters in the Flats, but you'll find that in any settlement. Residents on this side of the Cove aren't all lily-pure."

"But Daniel mentioned that a few children living there are eligible to attend our school," Marie said, somewhat distressed, "and he volunteered to take me to visit the parents. He didn't mention that it wasn't a safe place to go."

"Oh, Daniel isn't too careful in choosing his friends," Viola said, with a toss of her blond hair.

It was on Marie's tongue to retort, "Apparently

not, or he wouldn't have chosen you," when she thought of her mother's reaction to such a statement. Even though she'd just turned twenty-four years old, she wasn't too old to have her mouth washed out with soap if she'd made such a comment. Determined that she wouldn't become involved in a verbal battle with Viola, Marie opened the screen door into the house.

"Excuse me," she said. "I need to bathe and put on some clean garments."

"We won't have supper for a couple of hours," Lena said. "Take a nap if you want to. You'll have time."

Daniel's thoughts were troubled. He wasn't used to spending much time thinking about romantic pursuits, and he was annoyed when he thought about Marie the rest of the day. He was also disgusted with himself—he'd always been proud of his ability to control his emotions and just dwell on what he wanted to. Now that he'd met Marie Bolden, he couldn't get her out of his mind. He'd always laughed at men who said there was only one woman in the world for them, and Daniel had scoffed at their attitude. He'd never yet known any woman whom he considered indispensable. Could this beautiful young woman be the exception?

One thing was for certain: he wanted to see more of Marie. He decided that sharing a meal was a safe way to get to know a woman without seeming too interested in her. He didn't want to impose on his grandmother by going to her home to eat, so perhaps he could invite Granny and Marie to his home for a meal. Not one to delay, Daniel opened the front door and followed the long hall to the kitchen.

Brown Dove and her son, Matsu, had worked several years for him, and as usual he found her in the kitchen. "Hello, Dove, I'd like to invite Granny and the new schoolmarm to have a meal with me some evening, or maybe some Sunday afternoon. When would be a good time?"

"Most anytime, Mr. Daniel," Dove said, speaking English as well as Daniel's own.

"Then I'll invite them for this coming Sunday after church."

Nodding, Dove said, "What do you want me to fix?"

Laughing, Daniel patted her shoulder, "Anything you prepare will be wonderful. You're the cook— I'm not. I'll check with Granny to be sure they can come."

Pleased with himself and refusing to admit how much he was attracted to Marie, Daniel went to the phone, and wonder of wonders, he not only reached his grandmother on the first call, but she agreed to come.

"That is, if it's convenient for Marie," she qualified her statement. "I'll let you know after I talk with her tonight."

He couldn't tell from the tone of his granny's voice whether she was surprised. He'd never invited any other woman to have dinner with him. Well, let her think what she wanted to.

* * *

Throughout the next two days, as Lena guided her around the area to meet the families who would have children attending the school, Marie occasionally wondered why Daniel had invited her to his home. But she was so dismayed at the poor living conditions of many of the families that she didn't spend much time thinking about Daniel and the invitation.

Although Lena told her that the majority of the parents couldn't read, Marie had nailed to trees and fence posts several posters giving the school hours.

During those visits she learned that she would have twenty students, ranging in age from five years old to one girl who was eighteen. There were fifteen various-sized students' seats, which meant that some of the children would have to share a desk. She would have preferred that each student have a personal desk, but she wasn't going to complain to the trustees about the school's needs until she'd taught for a month or two. The books would be adequate unless they'd overlooked children who should be in school. Acting on Lena's advice, she would seat the boys on one side of the room, with an aisle to separate them from the girls on the other side.

When Marie commented on the parents' obvious interest in the education of their children to Lena, the former schoolteacher hesitated before she answered slowly, "Well, we haven't visited Chestnut Flats yet."

Surprised, Marie said, "But why would any parents object to their children having an education?

All children should have the opportunity to attend school."

"I believe that and you believe it," Lena said, "but…"

"But what?"

"Chestnut Flats is a notorious region of Cades Cove. Some of the residents moved into that area because they'd gotten into trouble with the law in towns hereabouts. Quite a few bootleggers live there, too. They avoid Cades Cove, and we're satisfied to keep it that way."

Marie mulled the situation back and forth in her mind, before she said, "That isn't fair for the children. I can already foresee that parents of some children who do come to school won't want their children to be in the company of those from Chestnut Flats. Whether they attend or not, I feel that I should at least give them an opportunity to do so."

Laughing, Lena said, "I knew you'd see it that way—that's why I've been debating whether or not to even mention it. You'll have a more peaceful school year if you don't stir up that hornet's nest. I agree that those children should not be neglected, but let's pray about it before you make a decision."

"Yes, my parents taught me to pray for guidance about any and all problems. A few times when I've not done so, I've lived to regret it. You're such a blessing to me, Lena. I thank God for placing you in my life."

"Well, you're a blessing to me, too! I lost my daughter when Daniel was a baby, and I still miss her. I love Daniel, and I certainly loved his father, too, but it's not the same as having a girl around. I just know we're going to have a wonderful school year."

Putting her arms around Lena's shoulders, Marie gave her a tight hug. "I'm very flattered. And I know Mother will consider that quite a compliment. I wouldn't be the sort of person you'd want to claim if it hadn't been for her love and guidance."

Marie had been accustomed to walking from their home in Canaan several times a week, but it seemed that since she'd been in Cades Cove, she'd ridden in the buggy or on horseback when she went anywhere. One afternoon, feeling the need for exercise as well as a time to meditate, Marie put on a jacket and told Lena she was going for a walk. She turned on the road toward Canaan and walked slowly, needing time to sort out her thoughts and sentiments about this move to Cades Cove.

Had accepting the teacher's position in the Cove been a mistake? She was dismayed by the over-whelming needs of the children she would be teach-ing. Could she make a difference in their lives? Could she relate to them when her life had been so different? Did she know how to teach children who were far behind the other children their age?

Having been taught by her mother at an early age that she shouldn't make any decisions without pray-ing for God's guidance in giving the answer, Marie believed that He had approved her move to Cades

Cove. Still, sometimes she wondered if she would have come if she hadn't wanted to see more of Daniel. After she'd walked and meditated for a mile or two, Marie was again convinced that God had approved her move. Could it be that He wanted her to be instrumental in leading Daniel to a different attitude concerning Him? What was to be her role in Daniel's life?

Although she was busy with preparations for the opening of the school season, Marie thought about the invitation from Daniel to visit his home. She'd gathered from a few comments made by Lena that the house was somewhat out of the ordinary in the Cove. Shaking her head, Lena had said, "I don't know what ever possesses Daniel to live in such a mansion alone. I thought he intended to marry Viola." Laughing lightly, she added, "I think Viola thought he would, too."

This comment startled Marie, and she'd said, "Would you welcome Viola as a granddaughter?"

"Not particularly, but I would like to have some great-grandchildren before I die. However, Daniel seems to be perfectly content as a bachelor."

Remembering the conversation she'd had with her father, and his desire for grandchildren, Marie said, "You remind me of Dad. He wasn't a bit happy when I agreed to come to Cades Cove as a teacher. I think he was sorry he'd sent me to college. I didn't like to disappoint him, but even as a child, I daydreamed about teaching school."

Glancing quickly at Marie, Lena said, "Does that

mean you intend to make a career of teaching? Don't you ever intend to marry?"

Marie didn't answer the question, saying instead, "I don't know that there's a law forbidding a married woman from teaching."

"But would you want to teach if you had children?" Lena asked.

"I wasn't thinking of myself in particular. My mother wasn't a teacher, but she spent many hours helping people with health problems. Of course, we had a cook and housekeeper, so that freed Mother to help those in the community who needed her."

After Marie had walked another mile or more, she sat on a fallen log beside the road and drew a deep breath. She couldn't believe that in the short time she'd been in Cades Cove she'd become so involved in the lives of the people. Having lived all her life in such a loving home and having two devoted parents, she had dreaded leaving.

Smiling, she remembered Aunt Fannie's comment. "You's got the best home in the world, missy, and I can't imagine what would make you want to leave it to teach school in some God-forsaken place like the Cove!"

Marie had tried to think of an explanation that would help Aunt Fannie understand why she wanted to teach school. Why she wanted some freedom. Aunt Fannie had been born into slavery, although Vance's family had granted her freedom even before the War Between the States. But with their background of servitude, the few blacks that were now in the employ of Evelyn and Vance considered themselves as belonging to the family.

"I don't know exactly why I want to show my independence, either," Marie had said, "but it's probably a trait I inherited from my parents. Now stop quarreling with me, Aunt Fannie, and give me a hug. Also, pray for me—I'm stepping out into the unknown, and I'm afraid."

Aunt Fannie had grabbed Marie and squeezed so tight that Marie had laughed and said, "You're about to crack my ribs. Don't hug me so tight."

"I's gonna miss you, but I'll pray that the good Lord will keep you safe. And don't forget—you've always got a home here."

Marie looked forward to the visit to Daniel's house because she'd learned from Lena that his home was a legacy from his grandfather. That Sunday, she and Lena traveled to the church in the buggy, and after the services ended, Lena turned in the opposite direction toward a wide hollow where Marie hadn't been before. It was only a short distance before Lena made a sharp turn that brought them in sight of a magnificent farmstead.

"Oh, my!" Marie gasped. "Is that where Daniel lives?"

Lena pulled the horse to a halt, while Marie stared mesmerized at a two-story frame house located on a slight knoll at the head of the hollow. It looked more like a Southern plantation home than what she would have expected to see in Cades Cove. "Yes, and it hasn't been a very happy home. As I've told you, his mother died when Daniel was still a babe. Daniel was older when his father passed away, but he's spoiled and doesn't live the way I would prefer. Considering his unfortunate childhood, it could be worse. I've sensed that Daniel blames God for the loss of his parents. I've tried to be a mother as well as grandmother, but I know he's very lonely."

"It's a beautiful home, and looks like many of the plantation homes I saw in South Carolina. Surely with such a heritage Daniel would want to have children to carry on the family name and run this beautiful farm."

With a pert glance in Marie's direction, Lena said, "I haven't given up yet. I believe I'm nearer to becoming a great-grandmother than I've ever been."

Marie felt a blush cover her face, but she said, "If I were you, I wouldn't count those great-grandchildren before they're hatched."

Chapter 3

Daniel must have been watching for them, for he waited on the front porch until Lena drove the buggy into the yard. He came quickly down the steps and motioned to a Cherokee youth who stood nearby. The Cherokee sauntered to the horse and held its bridle while Daniel helped his grandmother to the ground, then turned to lift Marie down. "Welcome to my home," he said as he steadied her.

"It's a lovely house, Daniel," Marie said. "It reminds me of the mansion where I stayed during my two years in Charleston. I can't believe I'm looking at a white-columned two-story brick mansion here in the mountains of North Carolina."

"I don't know too much about the history of the house, but it was built by my grandfather, who struck it rich in the California Gold Rush," Daniel explained. "It's a bigger house than I need, but it's a legacy that I cherish. I have a few Cherokee people who work for me and keep up the house and grounds."

Although Lena went inside, Marie stood on the porch and gazed in awe at the setting. "Why, the scenery is breathtaking. How fortunate you are to live here."

While Lena visited with the cook and helped with last-minute dinner preparations, Daniel took Marie on a tour of the house. When they stood on the second-floor balcony and enjoyed the scenery, Daniel said hesitantly, "Perhaps I'm going about this all wrong, but I'm not the most tactful person in the world or I wouldn't say this…but I have feelings for you that I've never experienced before, and I don't like it."

Marie glanced toward him and felt herself blush, but she laughed and said, "I'd prefer for you to comment further on that statement before I give an answer."

"For some reason," he said, "it seems that I often have one woman or another dangling after me. It's been that way since I was a boy. I like women well enough, but I don't want to get married, so I've never had a serious relationship with anyone. I thought I should tell you."

"Well, Daniel, if it will make you feel any better, I don't have any interest in getting married, either," she said, wondering if she was being completely truthful. "Frankly, not many school boards will hire women teachers. The only reason I got this job was because no one else wanted to teach in Cades Cove. And many school boards won't hire married women, either. So if you're suggesting that we should be friends only, you can be assured that I'm not going to try to trap you into marriage. I'm here to teach."

Daniel frowned and muttered, "I don't know that suits me, either."

Standing, Marie said, "When you make up your mind, you can let me know. In the meantime, I'm going inside to see if the women need any help."

Marie couldn't determine whether she was feeling anger or disappointment. One thing she did know—it was a sorry day for her when she met Daniel Watson.

Even before she started praying, Marie was convinced what God's answer would be. She recalled incidents when Jesus had fed the multitudes, and particularly remembered the time when the disciples had tried to send the children away from Him. Jesus invited the children to gather around Him, and reproved the disciples, "Suffer little children, and forbid them not, to come unto me—for of such is the kingdom of heaven." Marie was convinced that several of those children invited to come to Him were unlearned, dirty, poor and needy, just as the ones in Chestnut Flats were. But if the Savior of the world could lower Himself to help the poor, the handicapped and the outcasts of society, could she do less?

Accusing herself of being a coward, Marie didn't go the next day to call on parents in Chestnut Flats. Dressing in one of her oldest garments and, at Lena's insistence, tying a scarf around her head, she hitched the mare to the buggy and set out for the schoolhouse. Since the school had been closed for several months, everything would need to be dusted and scrubbed. She got proof of that the day she and Daniel had put her books and supplies in the room and she'd returned to Lena's covered in dirt. She also wanted to wash the windows before the first day of school. When she entered the building, she looked around helplessly, wondering how she'd ever get all of the work done.

Although the Boldens had always retained servants to do the housework, Marie's parents had insisted that their children learn to work. Marie had worked alongside their house servant, Aunt Fannie, a few days each month. At first she resented doing the work—now she was thankful that her mother had insisted that she learn to do manual labor. Evelyn had reminded her often of the hardships the Confederate women encountered during the war and after the conflict had ended—how formerly rich women had been at a loss to know how to perform the difficult tasks they found necessary for survival. Although Evelyn didn't expect her family members to ever be in such difficult circumstances, she wanted them to be prepared if it was ever necessary.

Now Marie knew that training hadn't been wasted. She'd learned a lot of tasks during those hours when she'd worked beside Aunt Fannie—one of which was to have compassion for the people who had to work just to keep food on the table. Although she had looked forward to getting married when she met the right man, she wanted to prove that she could take care of herself if it was necessary.

Against his will, her brother Earl had been forced to work in the fields with the men who farmed the Bolden acres. He resented the work, and when he was sixteen he had left home. Occasionally, they'd heard news of Earl and knew that he lived in a log cabin somewhere in the Smoky Mountains. Once or twice a year when he came to Canaan to buy food supplies, he stopped by his parents' home for a brief visit, but he never stayed overnight. She understood that he lived off the land and had an income from trapping. Marie hadn't seen him since she'd gone to college in Charleston two years ago.

As she often did, Marie wished that she had a closer relationship with her brother. She wondered why she and Earl weren't more alike. Being twins, one would have thought they would have been inseparable, but her brother apparently wasn't interested in keeping in touch with his family. She was glad to know he lived in the area and she hoped she would see him soon.

She hadn't been in the schoolhouse very long before the door opened and a smiling Lena walked in followed by Minnie Hofsinger, and another woman, introduced to her as Lizzie Crossen, the woman who lived nearest to the schoolhouse. They carried buckets, mops and brooms. Apparently amused at Marie's amazement that they'd come to help her, Lena said, "You didn't think we'd let you do all of this work by yourself, did you?"

Breathing a sigh of relief, Marie said, "I hadn't given it much thought, but I was beginning to feel overwhelmed, wondering how I could possibly get the room ready in time to start school."

"My home is just down the road a piece," Lizzie said. "In fact, I'm sort of a janitor. When it starts getting cold, I usually build a fire in the stove and get the room warmed up before the teacher shows up. Of course, we've mostly had men teachers, and most of them didn't know a broom from a mop, so the women had to keep the building clean." Appraising Marie from head to toe, she continued, "You don't look like you're used to doing much cleaning, either."

Marie was surprised by such a candid welcome, but she laughed and said, "I haven't done much, I'll admit, however, my mother was strict in her training. She was an orphan and was raised by nuns in England. And my father had fought in the War Between the States, so he also knew what hardships were. They wanted to be sure that if I ever needed to make my own way, I'd know how to do it, so they insisted that I must learn to keep house."

"Wise parents," Lena said.

"Yes, they are. I'll admit I resented having to work when I was a child, but as I grew older I saw the wisdom of it."

The three women were a tremendous help and soon they had the floor swept and mopped, the windows clean, and the furniture dusted and polished. Dainty white curtains hung at the freshly washed windows.

After the women left, with Marie's grateful thanks for their help, she continued to organize the room to suit her, storing books and other supplies in places that would be convenient for the children. She found a poem, "Four-Leaf Clovers," which had been copyrighted the previous year by Ella Higginson in a book titled *When the Birds Go North Again*. The poem was illustrated with the pictures of two girls and a boy playing in an open field, somewhat like the area around the school building. Marie read it aloud, slowly, remembering when she'd memorized poetry as a child, and decided it would be a good poem for her medium-age pupils to learn.

"I know a place where the sun is like gold,
And the cherry blooms burst with snow;
And down underneath is the loveliest nook,
Where the four-leaf clovers grow."

She'd enjoyed poetry, but Earl had always laughed when he heard her reciting a new selection. One day he'd accused her of sounding like a bleating sheep when she'd been learning a portion of one of William Shakespeare's sonnets.

Wondering if she would encounter Earl during her stay at Cades Cove, or if she would even recognize him if she did, Marie was startled by a knock on the door. She was standing on a stool, shelving some books, so instead of stepping down, she called, "Come in!"

A man opened the door and stepped inside. It

wasn't Daniel, as she'd expected, but a stranger. Heavily bearded and, with a hat pulled over his forehead, it was difficult for her to see his face. The man looked like a rough customer, and momentarily she was fearful, wondering if he was one of the men she'd heard about from Chestnut Flats. Leaning against the doorjamb, the man laughed jovially before he said, "Now I've seen everything! The spoiled daughter of Vance and Evelyn Bolden, dressed up like a servant and doing menial labor. What's happened? Did you get disinherited and have to take up cleaning for a living?"

Stepping off the ladder, Marie raised a couple of the window blinds so she could get a closer look at her visitor. He didn't look like anyone she'd ever known, but walking closer to him, she noticed that the man's eyes were exactly like her mother's.

"Earl?" she questioned, finding it difficult to believe that this broad-shouldered, bewhiskered man was her brother. When he'd returned from the fighting in Cuba in 1898, he was a near invalid, having been ill with malaria during his time in the tropics. After spending a few weeks at home and not improving, he'd decided to go to the Cherokee nation for healing. He'd heard all of his life about his mother's Cherokee friend, Taynita, who had been instrumental in saving his life when he was only a baby. She'd used herbs and other native methods to restore his health. He believed it was worth a try to see if the same treatment could cure him. Looking at the brawny, healthy man who stood before her, Marie knew that the treatment had been successful.

"Earl, is it really you? I was just now thinking of you and wondering if I would get to see you. I heard you live around here."

He grabbed her in a bear hug and squeezed her so hard that she couldn't breathe.

"Stop it," she mumbled. "I think you've cracked my ribs."

"Nonsense! You're a Bolden, remember? We don't bruise easily."

He lifted her and swung her around and around before he finally released her, and being dizzy she staggered to sit down in the nearest chair.

"Hey! I'm not a child anymore. Stop that. But I'm surely happy to see you. Tell me where you live. Is it far?"

"My home is on the nearest mountain—about two hours' walk away. It's on the edge of the Cherokee reservation. One of the natives told me that a woman by the name of Bolden had come to teach in Cades Cove. I was sure it wasn't Mother, but thought it might be you. What possessed you to come here?"

"No other community would hire me. Female schoolteachers are not popular in the Carolinas. Apparently teaching in Cades Cove isn't a job anyone else wants. When they approached me, I accepted right away because I didn't have answers from any of the other places where I'd applied."

Earl straddled a bench in the front of the school-room, facing Marie.

"But I still don't understand why you're teaching. It can't be that you *need* the money. Isn't Dad prosperous anymore?"

"Of course he is. But I wasn't content to sit at home, let my parents support me, and end up marrying somebody I didn't love just because it was expected of me. I've thought about it a lot—we have the same blood in our veins as our parents, and that's why we've chosen to make our own decisions about how to live. We're adventurous. Why didn't they stay in England, rather than risk a voyage across the Atlantic? When our father was killed in a shipwreck, our mother could have gone back to Europe but, no, she agreed to marry Vance Bolden and emigrate from Charleston to the mountains of North Carolina. Wanderlust is in our blood!"

Nodding, Earl said, "You're right, of course. And I have a feeling this school teaching isn't going to be an easy task, either."

"I don't expect it to be. But that's enough about me. What have you been doing with yourself? Mother prays daily for you and wishes you'd come to see her. Dad misses you, too, for that matter."

"I know I disappointed them, and people probably think I'm crazy for giving up the easy life to live in a log cabin in the woods. But I haven't been wasting my time." He walked to the door, opened it and scanned the area around the schoolhouse. Then he sat on a chair close to Marie, reaching into his pocket for a leather pouch.

"Hold out your hand," he said, and when she did

what he asked, he sprinkled some of the contents of
the pouch into her hand. The small chunks sparkled
brightly in the beam of sunlight that flashed through
one of the windows Marie had cleaned. She stared
at him, speechless.

"About a year ago, I found a small pocket of gold
on the land I bought from the Cherokee tribe. I've
been mining it off and on since then, and I have quite
a stash of gold. Besides that, I've managed to make
a good living from hunting and trapping in the win-
tertime. Now I've decided to use that money, settle
down, buy some farmland and raise a family, but
I'm not in any hurry. I want to be sure I make the
right decisions."

"Really? What caused you to change your mind?"

Smiling broadly, he walked to the door again. In
words that Marie supposed were Cherokee, he called
out while motioning with his hands. Soon a young
Cherokee woman stepped inside the door. She stood
with averted face, but Marie noted that she had soft,
dark skin. Her long black hair was wavy and neat.
Her head reached only as far as Earl's shoulder, but
the luminous shine in Earl's eyes as he looked at the
girl proclaimed his love for her.

"This is my friend Awinta, which means *fawn* in
English. We're going to be married in a traditional
Cherokee ceremony, but I intend to make it legal according to North Carolina's laws, too. Do you know
any of the preachers around here?"

Marie shook her head, while wondering what her

parents would think of the match. "I just arrived in the Cove not long ago myself."

Hearing a horse's hooves on the road, Marie looked out and saw Daniel approaching.

"Here comes the man who can tell you. He's a native of the Cove."

Earl glanced out the window. "Oh, that's Daniel Watson. I've seen him a few times around Canaan and Cades Cove."

Daniel dismounted in one fluid movement as he usually did and bounded up the steps. He stopped short when he saw Earl and Awinta.

"Oh, I'm sorry," he said to Marie. "I didn't know you had company."

"Daniel, this is my twin brother, Earl Bolden," Marie said, smiling. "As you know, I haven't seen much of him for the past few years. I intended to try and find him while I was at the Cove, but he saved me that trouble. This is his friend Awinta," she added.

The two men shook hands, and Daniel bowed slightly toward the Cherokee woman. Daniel glanced from Earl to Marie. "I can easily see the family resemblance. I thought you reminded me of someone I'd met before. As I mentioned, I've seen your brother a few times."

Smiling, Marie said, "Well, we *are* twins, though of course we're not identical, Earl being a man and all."

"Awinta and I are planning to get married," Earl explained to Daniel. "She wants the traditional Cherokee wedding, but I want to marry her in a church, too. We came to make arrangements for the wedding. My parents may not approve of our marriage, but it will be less bothersome to them if we have a church wedding, too. Awinta is a Christian, and we decided to be married in a church here in the Cove and have another wedding later on at the reservation."

"I can introduce you to one of the preachers," Daniel said. "Are you thinking that the local preachers will hesitate to marry you because of Awinta's Cherokee heritage?"

When Earl nodded, Daniel pointed at the church across the road. "That may be the situation in some instances, for there is some prejudice in the Cove against the Cherokee, but I feel sure the pastor of that church will marry you."

Awinta had said very little up until that time, but she spoke, and Marie was surprised at how well she spoke English. "I do not want to bring any trouble to Earl. I love him very much, but if our marriage will displease his people, I will not marry him."

Earl and Marie exchanged glances, and Earl shrugged his shoulders.

"I've told her that it won't matter one iota to our mother. However, I'll have to admit that Father might object," he said. "Since Mother was raised in England and came to this country as a missionary to the local Indian tribes, she will certainly approve. She'll convince Father that it's the right thing to do."

"That's true, but Father doesn't object to the fact that our mother's best friend is a full-blood Cherokee," Marie said, "so we'll pray that he will accept Awinta."

Marie stepped closer to Awinta and hugged her. "I, for one, will certainly do my best to make you a beloved member of our family. I'm looking forward to having you for a sister." Looking over the girl's shoulder, Marie met Daniel's glance, and he nodded approval.

"The preacher is clearing weeds from the cemetery across the way," Daniel said, "If you want me to, I'll go along and introduce you to him. I don't think he'll hesitate to perform the ceremony."

Earl nodded. He turned to Marie and said hesitantly, "I'd like for Mother and Dad to be here when we get married. I know Mother will want to attend, but I'm not sure that Dad will approve, so I don't suppose he will come to the wedding."

"I'm not so sure about that. Dad has mellowed a lot in the past few years," Marie said. "I think he'll come."

Marie stood in the doorway of the schoolhouse and watched as they walked the short distance to the church. Awinta was a small woman, and she was dwarfed by the two tall men who walked beside her. The pastor apparently agreed to perform the ceremony, for Awinta and Earl went into the church with him. When Daniel returned, he lounged on the bottom step and Marie sat beside him.

"Are they going to get married right now?" Marie said. "I'd like to have attended."

Shaking his head, Daniel said, "The pastor is just

counseling with them now, but Earl wants to invite your parents to be here, so the ceremony probably won't take place until the spring. Awinta wants a traditional Cherokee wedding, which will be held at the reservation after they're married here. Do you have any problem with that?"

"Of course not! It's obvious they're very much in love. It must be wonderful to find a person you love that much."

"I assume you've never found that person?" Daniel said, a solemn expression on his face. Without looking at her, he continued, "Or am I getting too personal?"

Marie's face grew warm, and she hoped that Daniel didn't notice her blushes.

"I can't answer that question because, if I have met that special person, I don't know it," she said. "I've heard the expression 'love comes softly,' which says to me that love between a man and woman doesn't necessarily hit the couple like a bolt of lightning. Rather love sneaks up on them in a slow and gentle manner. Perhaps that will happen to me."

He nodded solemnly and didn't look her way. Marie wanted to ask Daniel if *he* had found a special person, but remembering what Viola had hinted about her relationship with Daniel, she didn't want to know the answer.

Chapter 4

Since school was scheduled to start the following Monday, Marie spent the next few days preparing lessons and becoming oriented with the schoolroom and the textbooks that the children would use. According to the number of books, as well as the content, the school curriculum was apparently not as advanced as the school in Canaan. But, of course, Cades Cove didn't have the support of people like Evelyn and Vance Bolden, either.

That the school building and furnishings were somewhat inferior to what she'd known didn't discourage Marie because she hadn't expected the Cove's culture to be on a scale with Canaan.

Knowing that her mother would want to know every detail about the schoolroom, Marie sat at the teacher's desk and wrote a description of where she would be teaching. After telling her mother about seeing Earl, she looked around the room as she continued:

The building is boxlike, rectangular, about twenty-four feet by thirty feet, with windows along the sides, doors in front and back, ten-foot ceilings, wood framed and tin-roofed.

A potbelly stove sits in the middle of the room, just like the one in the schoolhouse in Canaan. The fuel for the stove is wood or coal. I hope it will keep the room warm enough during the winter. Many of the children I've seen so far are not adequately clothed.

The windows along the sides don't let in very much natural light except during certain times of the day. However, I intend to keep the doors open on fine days. If the children don't get too distracted by what's going on outside, that is.

The desks are simply made, four legs under a flat board. There is no other furniture. A wall map hangs on the wall behind the teacher's desk.

In the upper-right corner of the desktops is a hole for an inkwell or ink bottle to sit, just like the desks we had in the Canaan school. Pencils are penny cedar-covered lead with a small pointed rubber eraser. The slate pencil is a stone; round, with a paper covering to prevent breaking if dropped. Other supplies include a slate and tablet containing about fifty sheets of yellow paper ruled with lines. Copy books are available to the students who can pay ten or fifteen cents for them. I fear that many of my students may not be able to afford them, though. Perhaps we can think of a way to give each child one without it seeming like charity. The people here are very proud, like the people back home.

Now that we've cleaned the building and I've put away all the books and supplies I brought, the room is comfortable and pretty.

As she surveyed the room, Marie realized that the furnishings weren't much different from the school she'd attended as a child in Canaan. There were twenty pupils' desks, and each desk consisted of two parts. The seat could either be raised or lowered, and was attached to the front of another pupil's desk who sat immediately behind. The desks were lined up in rows and bolted to the floor, and each one was supplied with a handheld slate.

Remembering her days in school, Marie tried to devise a seating arrangement to keep any of the girls, who wore their hair in pigtails, from having them dipped in an inkwell by the boy who sat behind her. This had happened to her when she was in the first grade, and although her parents had paid little attention to the incident, Aunt Fannie had thrown a fit that one of her "chiluns," as she called Marie and Earl, would be so mistreated.

She placed a bench in front of her desk where she could have students sit when it was their time to recite or report on the current assignments for the day.

The blackboard seemed to be new, and she was pleased with that. In her childhood she'd used many blackboards that were in bad condition, and it had been a dreaded chore to write a sentence or a paragraph without a smooth surface beneath the chalk.

Still remembering her childhood, her thoughts turned to her twin. Poor Earl! He had never wanted to become involved in any of the activities in and around Canaan, and that was why he had finally disappeared, leaving only a note to the effect that he was going to the mountains to live with the Cherokees. Silently, she thanked God that Earl had found a wife and was apparently making a good living by farming and trapping—and prospecting. Their parents would be pleased, but she would let Earl inform them about his financial circumstances.

When the schoolhouse was ready for students, Mrs. Turner volunteered to take Marie to meet some of her prospective pupils from Chestnut Flats since she had already visited most of the other students in Cades Cove. Daniel came by the house that evening, and when his grandmother mentioned she was taking Marie to the Flats soon, he said, "Don't you think I'm the one to do that? Most of the people who live there are good citizens, but not all of them are."

"Oh, for goodness' sakes," Lena said. "Nobody is going to harm me. I've lived in this area most of my life, and I think I'm safe enough."

"I didn't have you in mind," Daniel said, with a stern glance at his grandmother. "There are some tough characters living in the Flats, and it might be well for them to see that Marie has male protection if she ever needs it."

Lena hesitated momentarily, but she said, "No doubt you're right. I'll take her visiting a few more places nearby. Then there's no reason you can't go along with both of us when we go to Chestnut Flats. That way, we can go anyplace we want to, without being afraid someone will harass us."

"I can do that," Daniel agreed immediately. "The crops at the farm don't need any attention now. Even if something comes up, my employees can handle anything necessary."

Somewhat distressed by this conversation, Marie wondered what kind of situation she'd brought upon herself. The longer she'd been here and the more she's heard about the Flats, the more she felt uneasy. Why hadn't she paid attention to her parents and stayed away from Cades Cove and Chestnut Flats? But she'd been so sure that it was God's will for her to come here that she hadn't considered the problems.

Her conscience pricked a little by causing her to wonder again if she was really seeking God's plan for her life or if she welcomed the opportunity as an ulterior motive to see more of Daniel Watson. Still, given her desire to teach and the scarcity of openings for female teachers, she knew she would have come to the Cove if she'd never met Daniel.

Besides, she didn't want to live in the shadow of the family's accomplishments all of her life. She wanted to prove that she could be self-sufficient. When she'd mentioned this sentiment to her mother, Evelyn had laughed knowingly. Giving Marie a hug, Evelyn said, "You inherited that independence from me. As an orphan, at an early age I realized that I couldn't depend on anyone except God to guide my steps. Considering everything, I feel more than satisfied with my life. And I think you'll find your way, too."

Perhaps noting the uncertainty and fear she was experiencing, Daniel put his arm around her shoulders in a brotherly hug. "Now, don't be worrying about this. Nobody is going to hurt you when they know they'd have me to deal with. But to be on the safe side, don't go to Chestnut Flats unless either Granny or I'm with you. Promise?"

Although she didn't like the idea of being obligated to Daniel Watson, she recognized the wisdom of his words, and she nodded agreement. Daniel and Lena's assessment of some of the residents in Chestnut Flats was probably the reason why her parents hadn't wanted her to take this job. Fearful as she was, however, she had spent several years of her life preparing to become a teacher. She wasn't going to give up her dream without making an effort.

The next afternoon Lena asked Marie to go with her to Chestnut Flats to pay a call on a destitute family that Lena often helped. Daniel wasn't available, but Lena felt it would be safe to go anyway. "This will give you a good introduction to that community before we visit the parents. Lots of good people there, but in any town or village, there will be citizens who aren't desirable. If I can help anyone, rich or poor, good citizens or bad, I go, and no one has ever threatened me yet."

She must have detected that Marie was growing somewhat skeptical about her teaching position and whether she'd be able to cope with the problems she was about to encounter. "I don't want you to be distressed by that warning Daniel gave you," Mrs. Turner said, as they approached the village. "Most of these residents are people who've lived in the area as long as I have, and you have nothing to fear from them. However, I'll have to admit that for the past year or so several newcomers, mostly men, have drifted into the Flats. They've built shacks on the edge of the settlement and pretty much keep to themselves. Daniel says that some of them will be gone for weeks at a time, so he thinks they may be involved in some kind of devilment in other areas and return here periodically to hide from the law. We don't have any proof of that, of course. He worries about me going there, too, but I have some friends in Chestnut Flats who need help from time to time, so when I'm needed I go." Smiling, she said, "Daniel needn't think he can boss his grandmother around."

Realizing that Daniel and his grandmother were much alike, she couldn't decide who was the boss in the family. She had the feeling that both of them did what they wanted to, and let the other one think it was his or her idea, but silently she thanked God for giving her the opportunity to know both Lena and her grandson. It amazed her that she had so quickly become fond of these people she'd known for such a short time. They'd made her feel cherished and protected.

The next afternoon, they visited several parents in the Flats whose children would be attending the school. Marie was gratified by their reaction. Most of the parents were enthusiastic, except for the families who lived in a questionable area of Chestnut Flats. Even there, they stopped at the home of one couple, Harry and Minnie Hofsinger, who invited them to stay awhile. Minnie had helped get the school building ready just a few days before, and Marie felt that she was already a friend. Marie quickly took advantage of the invitation to learn more about the home life of her prospective students.

The house was made of logs, pigs rooted in a nearby garden spot and the front porch was littered with farm equipment, harnesses and baskets, but when she and Mrs. Turner were invited inside the house, Marie was pleasantly surprised to find it neat and clean. The windows were covered with dainty white curtains and the furniture, while old, was enhanced by beautiful quilted coverlets and comfortable cushions.

"Why, this is a lovely room!" Marie exclaimed.

"I suppose you've made all of these beautiful quilts and cushions."

Obviously pleased, Minnie said, "Yes. My mother taught me to work with my hands, and it stood me in good stead when I married Harry and we moved to Cades Cove. I was very lonely at first, but I've learned to appreciate the solitude and this mountain air. We lived in the coastal area of Virginia, and it took some getting used to. I found the life hard at first, but I'm happy now."

Minnie called her two children in from playing to introduce them. "This is Sam. He's five," she said, ruffling the curly brown hair of a plump little boy. "He takes after my side of the family. Our girl, Rebecca, is a year older than he is. I'm so glad you're going to be here to teach them. I feared we might not find a teacher. Most of the people who live here are poor, and if a teacher can find something better, they won't come to the Cove. 'Course no one can blame them for that."

"I'll admit that my father didn't want me to come here to teach school," Marie said with a smile. "Actually, I felt that God was calling me to the Cove, and if that was so, He would provide a way for me."

"We're going to have a pie supper at the schoolhouse next Saturday night to get enough money to provide school supplies for all the children," Minnie said, changing the subject. "Have you ever been to a pie supper?"

Marie shook her head.

"The men bid on the pies the women make and

the winner gets to eat supper with the woman whose pie he bought," Lena added. "We usually have a big turnout. You'll have to make a pie—the men always like to bid on the teacher's pie, especially if she's as young as you are."

Laughing, Marie said, "I've *never* made a pie, so I'm convinced that no one would want a pie I made. At home, we have a cook who has been with the family since before I was born, and she won't let anyone else 'mess around in my kitchen,' as she calls it. Her bark is worse than her bite, though, so I've spent a lot of time watching her prepare our meals."

Marie didn't want it to seem like bragging to mention that her family had a servant to do the cooking, but she didn't intend to live under false pretenses, either. She hoped she would be able to prove that, regardless of her background, she was capable of teaching in a one-room school.

"You'll be expected to take a pie to this event," Mrs. Turner said. "I'll show you how to make one. We've seldom had women teachers here, and never one as young and pretty as you are. Your pie will probably bring a lot of money."

"I've never been to a pie supper, either, but it sounds like fun, and a good way for me to get acquainted with the parents. With your help, I'll make a pie or 'die a tryin',' " Marie said, quoting one of Aunt Fannie's slogans. "What kind of pie do you suggest I make?"

"Usually, the young woman makes a pie that she knows her special beau will want to buy. Chocolate pie is Daniel's favorite, in case you're interested," Lena said.

Shaking her head, Marie said, "Then I definitely won't make a chocolate pie. Viola will expect him to buy her pie."

"Then make something Daniel doesn't like," Minnie suggested.

Smiling, Lena said, "The only pie he doesn't like is pumpkin. He ate too much pumpkin pie once when he was a child, and he vomited all night. He can't stand the sight of a pumpkin pie since then."

"Then a pumpkin pie, it will be," Marie said.

"Are you getting excited about your work?" Lena asked as they headed for home.

"Very much so. Partly because I like to teach and because I want to be self-sufficient if the day comes when I have to work for a living."

"You're a wise woman," Lena said. "Your parents raised you right."

"They really did, and I appreciate it so much. You no doubt know about my parents' background. I feel that I must have inherited a little of their missionary zeal. I've concluded that my invitation to teach in Cades Cove is a special calling, too, and when I leave here, I'd like to know that I've made a difference in the lives of the children I've taught."

"There's no doubt in my mind that you'll do that," Lena assured her.

Although Marie had completed her teaching studies at the college with high honors, as the days drew nearer for the opening of school, she again began to doubt that she'd be successful as a teacher. The students she'd taught in her practice sessions at the college in Charleston had been the children or grandchildren of the professional staff. They were well-mannered, dressed in fashionable clothing and eager to learn.

As Lena took her to visit more of the homes, she observed the children of Cades Cove, and she didn't detect many of the characteristics she had encountered in her student teaching. The fact that many of the local children didn't have nice clothing didn't bother her nearly as much as their seeming lack of ambition.

When she bemoaned this fact to Mrs. Turner, Lena said, "Now, sit down and listen to me. I'm going to talk to you like your mother would do. You knew when you came here that this wouldn't be easy. Cades Cove is several years behind the rest of the world. Some of the children will be well behaved, well dressed and intelligent. Others won't. Their clothes may be patched, some of them may come to school dirty, they'll stink and there might be a few with lice in their hair."

"Lice!" Marie said, bewildered, having no idea what Lena was talking about.

"Head lice are small, bloodsucking insects. They live in the hair on people's heads and feed off the blood from their scalps," Lena explained.

A groan escaped Marie's lips. She felt light-headed and wondered if she was going to faint.

"I figured you'd never heard of them," Lena said, "so I wanted to warn you to be very careful about touching your hair while you're working with the children. Most of them will be clean, but some of the children only have one outfit, so they have to wear the same clothes every day. Their mothers will wash their garments on Saturdays."

Marie had the sensation that her scalp was crawling with vermin, and Lena must have felt sorry for her, because she said kindly, "If you don't touch your hair, you'll probably be all right, and I intend to check your hair every evening to be sure you haven't picked up any unwanted visitors."

Marie muttered, "It isn't possible," and shook her head in despair.

"It *is* possible, and likely to happen. I taught school here for several years," Lena continued, "and I know what you're facing. Nothing is going to be like it was in Charleston, or even in Canaan for that matter. If you aren't willing to accept that, now is the time for you to decide, and go back home, where everything is easy for you."

Tears welled up in Marie's eyes, and she ran from the kitchen and into her bedroom. Collapsing on the bed, she stared at the ceiling, wishing she'd never heard of Cades Cove. Why hadn't she been content like most other young women to get married and have children for someone else to teach? What was she trying to prove?

After she'd lain there for a half hour or so, she

heard a tap on the door. Knowing it was Lena, she said, "Come in."

With a slight smile on her face, Lena entered the room. "I supposed you'd have your clothes packed ready to head for Canaan by this time."

"You won't get rid of me that easy. When I encounter some of these situations you're mentioning, then I may give up and go home, but if I do, I'd be angry at myself the rest of my life. I may fail at being independent, but I'm not ready to call it quits yet."

"Good girl!" Lena said. She leaned over the bed and gave Marie a motherly hug. "You've got what it takes to succeed in this world."

"It's not me that I'm worried about, but I was thinking how terrible it must be for these children to live in such primitive conditions. How can I help them improve their way of living without sounding condescending?"

Marie sensed that Lena was watching her with a strange gleam in her eyes. "Now what have I said wrong?" she asked.

"Nothing wrong! I was just wondering how Evelyn and Vance Bolden raised a young woman like you. Anyone would be proud to have a daughter like you."

Somewhat embarrassed, Marie said, "Why thank you! I'll tell them what you said."

When Marie rang the bell on the first day of school and unlocked the door, she was amazed to see a large crowd of children on the lawn. The girls were giggling, and the boys engaged in a little horse-play as they crowded into the room, the boys sitting in the chairs on the left, and girls on the right. The boys pushed and shoved as they tried to claim seats until Marie, remembering Lena's advice, said harshly, "Stop that, or I'll assign you to the seats you'll be using."

She recalled Lena's farewell words that morning.

"I'll pass along the same advice that one of the trustees gave me when I started teaching—don't let the students see you smile for a week or more. If you'll establish who's boss during the first few weeks, the school year will be bearable. If you don't, the older kids will make your life miserable. I'm not saying it will ever be easy, because you'll face new challenges every day. I don't mean to discourage you," Lena said. "You'll do all right. At least ninety percent of the parents will support what you're doing."

Groaning, Marie said, "I probably won't last through the first week."

"Oh, yes, you will," Lena said. "We'll pray you through those difficult days."

Unfortunately, the previous teacher hadn't left a list of students, or even what grades she would be expected to teach, so the rest of the morning was consumed as Marie learned the names of her students and what grades they were in. With their help, books were distributed and Marie breathed a sigh, feeling that she was making a good start to the school year.

Although lacking in many items that Marie

thought indispensable to a school, one of the things that surprised her most was that there wasn't an American flag in the building. Fortunately when she'd been packing the books she had brought to the Cove, she'd come across a flag of the United States of America. Evelyn had bought it once to display on the Fourth of July, but since Vance hadn't yet completely adjusted to the fact that the Confederates hadn't won the Civil War, she'd put the flag away.

Evelyn was pleased to have Marie take the flag with her, and she had hung the flag in a prominent place in the schoolroom, intending to start each day with the salute to the flag. Lena agreed that, when the Cove had such a diverse population from many sections of the country, it would be appropriate to display the flag. Knowing this, Marie didn't believe there would be any objection to starting the day with a salute to the United States, which was common in many schoolhouses around the country now.

Before she introduced her students to the salute, she wanted to be sure they understood the meaning of what they were reciting. She explained that several years earlier, a Boston-based youth magazine had published a twenty-two-word recitation for schoolchildren to use during planned activities to commemorate the four-hundredth anniversary of Columbus's discovery of America. Marie had done quite a lot of research on the recitation, and she'd decided that it would be appropriate to start the school day by having the students recite the pledge. She had written the words on the board.

So after she'd dealt with the preliminary registration and seating arrangements, Marie said, "I want to start each school day by pledging allegiance to the American flag."

A small hand shot up in the air from the row where two third-grade boys sat. "What's *allegiance?*" he said, stumbling over the word until it sounded more like *alesneezelance* to Marie.

"That's not quite the correct pronunciation," Marie said. "Let's learn to pronounce the word correctly first, then I'll tell you what it means. Repeat after me. Allegiance."

After several attempts to pronounce the word, all the students except a few of the younger ones said the word correctly. The words *allegiance* and *indivisible* seemed difficult for them, and Marie said, "Repeat after me."

Saying one line at a time, she waited for the students to repeat after her.

"I pledge allegiance to my Flag, and to the republic for which it stands: one nation indivisible with liberty and justice for all."

After explaining that *allegiance* meant loyalty to, or support for a person, cause or group, and that *indivisible* meant impossible to be divided by a given number, she asked the students to write the pledge in their notebooks. Their first assignment was to memorize the words, which they would say each morning when class started.

"Being loyal to our country is one of the most important things we can do as citizens," Marie explained, "and I hope that you will not only memorize these words as a way of opening each day's session, but that you will also consider them a promise to your country. I'll keep the words on the blackboard until you've memorized them. Now I'd like to tell you how this pledge became popular."

One of the boys raised his hand, and although Marie wanted the students to feel free to ask questions, she thought of all the activities she'd planned for the day. Which was the most important? To get to know her students by having them share their thoughts, or follow a plan that might not suit them at all?

Since she hadn't yet associated her students' names with faces, and not knowing all of the children's names yet, she nodded for the boy to continue.

"We've got some men in the Cove who're loyal to their country. Do you know Daniel Watson?"

"Yes," Marie answered, wondering where this was leading. "I live with his grandmother."

"Well, he went off to fight the Spanish when they tried to take over Cuba."

Another hand shot up. "There's a man who lives in the mountains near the Cherokee reservation who fought in that same war. His name is Earl something or other."

Smiling, Marie said, "Yes, I know. He's my twin brother—Earl Bolden."

The surprise on the boys' faces was amusing, and

Marie sensed that her popularity had shot up a notch or two. It was no small achievement, in their eyes, to have a brother who'd actually fought in a war.

One of the older boys said, "Maybe he'd come and talk to us someday about the fighting. Most of our teachers have special people visit sometimes."

"When I see him, I'll ask him to speak to us. As a matter of fact, I haven't seen him much for the past few years, so I'd also like to hear him talk about his experiences. Now, let me tell you about the Pledge of Allegiance and why I want you to learn, not only the words, but why it's important. I've written the words on the blackboard. Please copy them in your notebook."

Dutifully, the children copied the words, and when they'd finished, Marie explained, "Pledging loyalty to someone means promising to follow them—that sort of thing. There are many pledges people take throughout their lives, such as when a couple marries, when a man enters the armed forces of the United States or when a religious vow is taken."

Following the advice she had received from Daniel and Lena, the first day of school was dismissed at noon, and she had the afternoon to get a roll book completed. She had twenty-one students from the ages of five to eighteen, and she tried to determine how to teach diverse subjects to so many students. Lena had suggested that it was appropriate to ask some of the older students to help with the younger children, but Marie decided to try and keep the students busy enough that they wouldn't have time to help others.

Marie soon learned that the education of her oldest student wouldn't be easy. Although the girl was eighteen years old, she wasn't much more than on a fourth or fifth grade level. She faced another problem when she'd realized she had four children in the fifth grade, and there weren't enough books for each child to have a copy of his own.

The youngest child was Sam Hofsinger, the five-year-old boy whom she and Lena had visited in Chestnut Flats before the school year started. His heavily lashed gray eyes sparkled with pleasure that he was in school. Considering the distribution of books and the difficulty of learning the names of the students, Marie considered that the first week bordered on chaos.

After crying herself to sleep each night for the rest of the week, and doubting that she would ever be a competent teacher, she sent a call for help to her parents.

Though she already felt like a total failure by the end of her first week, Marie looked forward to Sunday so she could attend worship at the nearby church. Since there were several churches in the Cove, Marie had assumed that none of the churches would have a large attendance, thus she was pleasantly surprised when she and Lena arrived to find the churchyard full of buggies and saddled horses, as well as two horseless carriages.

The pastor's message, based on a Scripture passage from the book of Ecclesiastes, seemed to have been prepared especially for her.

The opening responsive reading included words written by King Solomon. Marie considered the words prayerfully. "Whatsoever thy hand findeth to do, do it with thy might." She could almost hear her mother saying amen.

The text of the pastor's sermon seemed to have been chosen especially for Marie's needs: Hebrews 11:8-9. "By faith Abraham, when he was called to go out into a place which he should after receive for an inheritance, obeyed; and he went out, not knowing whither he went. By faith he sojourned in the land of promise, as in a strange country, dwelling in tabernacles with Isaac and Jacob, the heirs with him of the same promise: for he looked for a city which hath foundations, whose builder and make is God."

As she had done often in the past few weeks, she compared her own life to the tenets of this verse.

Ten days after receiving Marie's letter, Vance and Evelyn arrived in Canaan with several boxes of books and more pencils and notepaper, which caused her to smile. No doubt her mother had bought the supplies when the school year had started and had them available if Marie needed them.

When she saw the abundant supply of books, Marie threw her arms around her mother, and her eyes filled with tears. "I've always thought you were a miracle worker, and now I know it. Where on earth did you find so many books in such a short time? I figured you would have to order my supplies from Raleigh or Columbia."

Evelyn drew Marie into a warm, comforting embrace, and laughing in her easy, confident manner, she said, "I canvassed every home in Canaan, begging for these books. Some of the owners want their books returned, and I've sent an order to Columbia to replace them."

Giving her mother another hug and a kiss on the cheek, Marie said, "Oh, Mama, you're the best mother any girl could have. I love you!"

Smiling, Evelyn said, "I suspected that you did, but it's always good to hear you say so."

Since there wasn't a reputable hotel in the Cove, Lena had insisted that Marie's parents should stay at her house. Marie gladly gave up her bed to her parents and slept on the davenport.

"So," Evelyn said, the next morning, "What do you think of your soon-to-be sister-in-law?"

"She's a beautiful young woman, well mannered and very much in love with Earl. I could readily see why he fell in love with her." Lifting her eyebrows and lowering her voice, she said, "More important, what does Papa think about the marriage?"

"As you might imagine, he threw a fit to find that we were to have a Cherokee Indian for a daughter-in-law, but he's finally accepted the fact that Earl is a man now and can make his own decisions. Indeed, your father has mellowed considerably in the past years, and he's overcome most of his prejudices, but I don't believe he'll ever come to terms with the

Confederate defeat, which was so devastating to his family."

"I realize that the War Between the States changed his life completely," Marie said, "but I find it difficult to see why it should have an impact on the way we live now, but it does. Even here in the western part of the state, which suffered very little destruction, there are still some people who've never 'surrendered,' if you know what I mean."

Evelyn nodded, and explained, "It wasn't so much the war itself, but the aftermath when certain political leaders in the North decided that the Southerners should be punished because they started the war, that caused the most ill will between the two sections. As an outsider, it's my opinion that the cause of the war wasn't one-sided, but those Reconstruction years were worse for the Confederates than the war itself. The Yankees were determined to punish the Southerners for starting the war, and the anger is still evident in many areas. I pray daily that something will occur to bring the two sections together again."

"Didn't that happen to some extent during the recent war, when soldiers from the North and the South invaded Cuba to drive out the Spanish?"

"Indeed it did." Laughing, Evelyn said, "Only recently, I read a newspaper article, recounting the incident of one former Rebel soldier who was fighting his way up San Juan Hill in Cuba. He turned to a comrade by his side, belted out a Rebel yell and said, 'Come on, boys. We've got them Yankees on the run.'"

Chuckling, Marie said, "That was probably Earl or Daniel Watson. They both fought in the Spanish-American War, as it's being called now."

Favoring Marie with a piercing glance, Evelyn said, "Perhaps I shouldn't even mention this, but every time you mention Daniel's name, your eyes brighten and a smile hovers on your lips. I sense that you're becoming fond of each other. Do you mind if I ask the nature of your relationship? Are you friends? Mere acquaintances? Or...?"

Shaking her head, Marie said, "I don't know! Don't apologize for asking me. I've wanted to talk to you about my attraction to Daniel, for it seems he's interested in me, too, but he doesn't share his grandmother's spiritual beliefs. Regardless of what my heart tells me, I don't intend to get involved with any man who doesn't share my Christian faith."

"It humbles me to know that I've been helpful in guiding you. Just keep focusing on what you believe the heavenly Father wants in your life, and you'll have the strength and wisdom to make the right decisions."

Chapter 5

Marie had been warned by both her mother and Lena that she must be careful not to have any favorites among her students, and she was determined that she wouldn't. However, as she settled into the first few weeks of teaching, Marie felt more and more drawn to Sallie Andrews, a ten-year-old girl who lived in Chestnut Flats. Although the child wore ragged garments, they were always clean, and of all the students, she seemed eager, almost desperate, to excel in any assignment Marie gave her. Marie soon learned it wasn't easy not to have favorites.

When Marie asked Lena if it would be appropriate for her to buy garments for the girl, Lena answered with a definite, "No! That would be considered playing favorites among your students. And so many children in Chestnut Flats need clothing."

Marie shook her head. "Not playing favorites is easier said than done, isn't it?"

With a militant gleam in her eyes, Lena said, "But there's nothing that says *I* can't take some clothes to her. What size do you think she wears?"

"You're asking a poor source for information," Marie said with a grin. "There haven't been any children in our family since Earl and I were born. But Sallie's head comes about to my waist, if that will give you an idea."

Lena was already searching through the shelves in her bedroom where she had enough fabric to provision a small store. "What colors do you think she would like?"

"She has dark blue eyes and black hair. I think she would look good in any of your fabrics."

"Both her parents are drunkards, so the child must have a horrible home life. I've given them clothes before, but they might resent a stranger 'messin' in' their business. It would definitely be better for you if the clothes came from me."

"That's fine." Marie gave Lena a tight hug. "God was certainly good to me when He directed me to your home. Already in the short time I've been here, you've kept me from making several mistakes. The next time I write to Mother, I'll ask her to order some fabric to replace what you're using."

"Aw, there's no need to do that," Lena objected.

"I know there isn't," Marie said. Grinning, she

added, "We Boldens are proud people, and we like to pay our way. Will you take the clothes to Sallie? Or may I?"

"Both of us will go," Lena said.

But when Daniel learned of their plans, he said, "As I told you before, neither one of you has any business going to Chestnut Flats. Several new people have moved in recently, and I don't trust them. *I'll* take the clothes."

Frowning at her grandson, Lena said, "And I suppose you'll be comfortable taking petticoats, night-gowns, underwear and the like to Leroy Andrews's little girl. He's got a suspicious mind, and he's liable to shoot you."

"Goodness!" Marie muttered. "I don't want to cause any trouble for Sallie—or for anyone else. I just want to help."

"And you *can* help, if we go about it the right way. But we have to think through this carefully. How about if you *and* Granny take the presents to Sallie? You can go in the buggy, and I'll ride along as your escort." Looking pointedly at Marie, he said to his grandmother, "If someone should insult *her,* we could get involved in a terrible ruckus."

"Oh, just forget it," Marie said wearily. "I don't want to start another Civil War."

"As long as I'm with you," Daniel asserted, "there *won't be* any trouble."

A few days later when Lena had finished making two dresses, a coat and several changes of underclothes for Sallie, Daniel came prepared to escort them to Chestnut Flats. Riding a magnificent chestnut horse, he was dressed in black garments, and he had two pistols strapped around his waist.

As she climbed into the buggy seat beside Lena, Marie gasped when she saw the weapons.

"Don't be alarmed," Daniel said, "This is just a warning. I'm not intending to shoot anyone, but the hoodlums in the Flats know that I could and would."

Speaking to Lena, he said, "I'm still not sure you two women should go to Chestnut Flats today. There's trouble brewing."

Turning a sharp glance in his direction, Lena said, "You can always find trouble there. What now?"

"Sallie's mother was killed in a drunken row last night."

Marie moaned and felt so light-headed that she feared she might fall out of the buggy. Daniel must have thought so, too, for he swung out of the saddle and was by her side immediately.

"Put your head down on your knees," he advised.

Shaking her head, Marie said, "I'm all right, but that poor child! Her life is bad enough already. What will happen to her?"

Lena said, "Let's go see what we can do. Daniel, it's a good thing you're going with us."

By the time they reached the small settlement, Marie had recovered her equilibrium, but she remained silent. She'd never been involved in such a tragedy before, so she felt it would be best for everyone if she remained silent. A large crowd had gathered around the log-cabin home, and Marie stayed in the buggy and held the horse's reins while the crowd made way for Lena to go inside.

Daniel dismounted, tied his horse to a nearby hitching post, stood beside the buggy and kept a continual eye on the people who whispered to one another as they waited for news of the killing. In a short time, Lena came out of the cabin, holding Sallie's hand.

Marie had been fond of Sallie from the first day she'd entered the schoolroom. Her work had been inferior compared to that of the other children of her age, but so eager was she to learn, she advanced rapidly. She was a pleasure to teach. She apparently had very little clothing, as she wore the same garments every day. Marie wondered what effect this tragedy would have on Sallie's life. Would it be better or worse in the future?

Sallie leaned against Marie when she got into the buggy, and Marie pulled her into a close embrace, feeling inadequate to know what to do. She didn't know what to say, either, so she remained silent, fearing she would say the wrong thing. Lena set a good example by talking calmly about the flowers along the roadway, the pleasant air and what she intended to prepare for supper.

When they arrived at Lena's home, Lena took Sallie into her bedroom and waited until the child went to sleep. In the meantime, Marie washed the dishes they hadn't had time to wash before they went to the Flats.

Marie poured water from the teakettle and stirred in some liquid soap that Lena had made. As she washed the dishes, her mind kept wandering to what a traumatic situation it was for Sallie to experience. As she'd grown into her teens, Marie had started to notice how her parents loved and cared for her and Earl and compared it to many other children of their age. Not that she and her brother weren't disciplined, but she knew instinctively that her life was easier than that of many of her schoolmates.

When the child went to sleep, Lena came downstairs and Marie poured a cup of coffee for her. Marie sat beside Lena at the table, but she didn't ask any questions at first. When Lena seemed more relaxed, Marie said, "What's going to happen to the child now?"

"I'll keep her with me for the time being. Her maternal grandparents live in a small town south of Canaan, and I'm sure they'll give her a home. I don't know them too well, but well enough to believe that they'll be good to Sallie. In the meantime, I'll keep her with me. I'm going upstairs now and be sure I'm there when she awakens."

In a short time, Lena returned, holding Sallie's hand. Her eyes were still red and swollen from crying and the nap she'd taken, but she nestled on Lena's lap and grabbed the jelly sandwich that Marie gave her. The way the child gobbled the sandwich was indicative of the home life the child had lived. When she went to sleep again, Lena laid her on the couch in the living room, and she and Marie sat nearby, with Lena holding the child's hand.

"If you think you can manage to stay alone with her for a short time, I'm going to find Daniel. I'll ask him to leave right away and inform Sallie's grandparents what has happened. She won't be a stranger to them because Sallie and her mother stayed with them for several months when the husband/father was in prison."

"Of course, I'll manage." Smiling slightly, she added, "I know a lot more about dealing with children than I did when I first came to Cades Cove."

It was a week before Sallie's grandparents came eagerly to Canaan to get their granddaughter. During that time Marie learned more about dealing with children than she'd ever believed was possible. When they arrived, Sallie's relatives made a good impression on Lena and Marie. They were obviously godly people, and from the clothes they wore and the horses and carriage they drove, they were affluent. It was obvious they weren't strangers to Sallie either, for they accepted her warmly and she seemed comfortable with them. With a mixture of both joy and sadness, Lena and Marie watched as Sallie was taken away from them.

The two women were convinced that the child would be safe in her grandparents' care, but they also knew that Sallie's absence would be difficult for them to accept. They went inside the home, sat on the sofa and with their arms around one another, cried as they shared the pain of losing the company of the child they'd learned to love.

Since Marie had never known her grandparents, she felt almost as if Lena was her grandmother, and it was gratifying to find that God had led her to board in the home of a woman who was as devout as her own mother. Each night, before going to bed, she and Lena knelt to pray.

One night, Lena said, "I hope you'll forgive me for mentioning this, but I sense that you and Daniel are romantically interested in each other."

Marie felt her cheeks grow warm, and she covered her face in her hands.

Continuing as if she wasn't aware of Marie's discomfort, Lena said, "You obviously don't approve of his current lifestyle. I've sensed that you are attracted to him, but are hesitant about letting him know it."

"That's true," Marie mumbled, lowering her hands and looking at Lena. "For several reasons, I'd like to see more of him so that I could be a witness about becoming more active in the Lord's work. I wonder why he doesn't go to church. You've certainly set a good example for him."

Sighing, Lena said, "In many ways, he's a wonderful man, and I'd like to think that the two of you might become interested in one another. Sometimes I think that he blames God for the fact that he lost his parents at an early age. He was not fully grown when his father died. I wanted him to live with me, but he wouldn't."

"I'll admit that I'm drawn to him," Marie said, "but my parents are very strict in their beliefs, and I know they wouldn't approve of me having a serious relationship with anyone who doesn't share the same Christian values that have molded my life."

"And I wouldn't want you to. Daniel knows the way he should live, but he's stubborn and he ignores all of my efforts to turn him toward the Lord. I love him so much and I want to see him become a believer before I die, but I don't witness to him anymore because it just irritated and drove him farther from changing his lifestyle. I just keep praying, believing in His own time, God will draw Daniel to Him. I only hope that I'm still alive when that happens."

"I've sensed your concern, and I want you to know that I, too, pray for his salvation. I've heard people say that prayer is the least we can do, but I believe that praying is the *most* we can do."

Lena nodded her agreement. "I've tried to teach Daniel the right way to go. I took him to church until he refused to go anymore. His father, who married my daughter, inherited a fortune his father made in the California gold fields, and Daniel being the only child, inherited all of that money when his parents died. He bought more land adjoining the original farm and stayed in his father's house on his own. He's always been good to me, and I don't have any control over what he does, but I pray that God will convict him of his wayward beliefs."

"I certainly agree with you. I'm not encouraging his attention, but it does make it awkward when I sense that he has more than a casual interest in me," Marie said. "Besides, I don't want to make enemies here in the Cove, and I know that Viola is interested in Daniel. She's your friend, so I probably shouldn't say this, but I suspect she could be a difficult adversary. If she thinks Daniel is attracted to me, she could cause me a lot of trouble. My parents would be very disappointed if I get involved in some kind of a scandal and lose my teaching position. I don't know her well, but I've heard some of the women who've helped at the schoolhouse discussing her attitude about living in the Cove and her proprietary attitude toward Daniel."

"I don't think you have anything to worry about," Lena assured her. "In the first place, it's my opinion that Daniel has no serious involvement with Viola. She's the one who makes all the overtures. I know he isn't perfect, and he keeps company with her because she pursues him, but he isn't interested in a permanent relationship with anyone. Regardless of their feelings for each other, Viola will never marry a man who won't take her away from Cades Cove, and I can't see Daniel living elsewhere." Laughing, Lena said, "Maybe we should pray, asking God to send a rich man into our midst—someone she will want more than she wants Daniel."

Smiling, Marie said, "I'll give it some consideration."

Since she'd never been involved in a pie supper before, Marie persuaded Lena and Lizzie to take charge of organizing the affair. When they met to discuss the plans, Marie thanked them again for their support, and said, "I'm not only inexperienced as a teacher, I'm even more unaware of Cove customs. I don't remember that we ever had a pie supper in Canaan. Please make the arrangements and tell me what I should do."

"We'll do that," Lena said. "First of all, you'll have to stand at the door and greet those who come."

"That shouldn't be difficult," Marie said. "My parents taught me to be friendly to everyone."

"And be sure you listen to the family names, as well as the first names, of those who come," Lizzie cautioned. "One thing that makes it hard for newcomers is that there's a lot of intermarriage in the Cove, and you have to be very careful of what you say about students. Anybody you mention would probably be a relative to several others. Learn your students' names and their relationship to each other, as soon as possible."

Marie threw up her hands in despair. "There's no way I can know the names of people who'll be here tomorrow night."

"You won't have to," Lizzie assured her. "You already know Lena and Daniel. They'll introduce you to people."

But in spite of the advice from Lena and Lizzie, Marie's nerves were on edge as time approached for the pie supper.

Although Marie had lost some sleep over it, with Lena standing beside her, giving instructions and watching every move she'd made, Marie had finally produced a pie that at least looked edible. Compared to the pies Lena made, Marie knew that it was far from perfect, but surely someone would want to buy it. By the time they left for the schoolhouse, Marie was so nervous that she didn't know whether she was afoot or on horseback. Actually, it wasn't either one, for she rode beside Lena in her buggy.

Lena suggested that Marie needed to arrive early, so they started to the schoolhouse more than an hour before seven o'clock, the time the function was scheduled to begin. As Lena's team trotted along the road, Marie prayed silently for the strength to get through the night without making any tragic mistakes. How she wished for her mother's presence to encourage her! Of course, Lena would be there, and although she had become almost like a grandmother, Marie needed encouragement from her parents. A large number of people were milling around in the schoolyard when they arrived, and Daniel stood on the steps.

"There's my boy!" Lena said with evident pride. "Daniel said he would arrive early and keep everyone out until we got here. The other two trustees have keys, too, and he knew they might open the doors too early."

"Yes, of course. That was thoughtful of Daniel."

"Daniel has his faults, but he really is a wonderful man. The woman who marries him will be blessed. I pray that he will find the right person and get married soon."

"You'd better hope then that he will find a woman who wants to provide the grandchildren you're longing for," Marie said with a smile.

"Which wouldn't be Viola! I don't doubt that she would agree to have children, but she wouldn't really be a mother to them. They would have a nanny, and although I know most nannies are wonderful with children, I believe children thrive best on a mother's love."

"Mother would agree with you. She was very attentive to Earl and me. She left us with Aunt Fannie, of course, but only for short periods of time. If she went with Dad on an overnight trip, she always took us with them until we were past twelve years old."

A couple of men met them in front of the school building and took charge of the horse and buggy by driving the buggy to the area where the vehicles were gathered.

Marie had intended to stand at the door and greet people as they arrived, but when several families crowded into the building at the same time, she started circulating among the parents and visiting with them. She was uneasy when she noticed that two of the guests were men she'd seen when Daniel had taken her on a tour of Chestnut Flats. They looked at her with speculative expressions on their faces that made her skin crawl. One man, in particular, Charlie Smith, made her uneasy. Although his attitude seemed all right, she mistrusted him, especially since he stood too close to her when he came to her side to talk about his son Josh who was in the third grade.

"Don't be afraid to lay the strap on him if he gets unruly," he said. "I've always told my kids if they get a whoopin' at school, they'll get another one when they get home. Ain't there a sayin', 'spare the rod and spoil the child'?"

"Yes, but I believe if you keep children busy working on their lessons, they won't have much time to misbehave. I don't anticipate whipping any of the students."

Erupting into a sound that Marie could only consider a horse laugh, he said, "I'll give you another week before you have to whoop somebody."

Fortunately, at that time, another family entered the building, so Marie turned to greet them, and Mr. Smith moved away. Unaware that Daniel had observed the encounter, she breathed easier when he stopped by her side and said quietly, "I'm keeping my eye on those two. Don't let them worry you. The first sign of trouble and out they go."

"Thank you. That makes me feel a lot better, for I'd really be upset if we have a brawl of some kind during the first entertainment I planned. Regardless, I won't permit them to get too familiar with me. I intend to maintain a good learning and fellowship environment here. I want the children to feel safe and content when they come to school, so I'll avoid any trouble with the parents if possible."

Daniel's fingers closed around her right hand, and he said quietly, "You go ahead and enjoy yourself and get acquainted with the visitors. If those two men become obnoxious, I'll politely, and quietly, invite them to leave."

Evidently Viola had seen that exchange, for she appeared suddenly beside them. "What are you two planning?" she said.

Startled, Marie took a few steps away from Daniel, and she tried to remove her hand from his, but his grip tightened.

"No plans," Daniel said. "I'm surprised that you had time to notice what we were doing, since you were so busy entertaining our guest."

Arching her eyebrows, Viola said, "Don't tell me you're jealous."

"Hardly that, Viola. Don't flatter yourself."

Irritated that Viola's insinuation had flustered her, Marie said, "I'll check with Lena now and see what the next move is."

"I can tell you that," Viola said. "It's time to start selling the pies. I counted, and there are thirty pies. Although that isn't as many as we usually have, it will take some time to complete the sales. Daniel, Mother made my pie. It's mincemeat, in a blue metal pan. What kind of pie did you make, Teacher?"

Fortunately, at that moment Lena motioned for Marie, and she gladly walked to where Lena sat at the teacher's desk ready to keep count of the pies sold and collect the money and the names of the highest bidders.

Taking Daniel's arm, Viola said, "Come and meet our guest. He's swarming with money and will probably buy two or three pies. He'll try to outbid you for my pie, Daniel."

Although she was already standing beside Lena, she heard Daniel answer, "That's all right with me. He's a guest, so we'll want him to feel at home. Introduce us, if you will."

"This is John Simpkins," Viola said. "He's a friend of Papa's from Richmond, Virginia." Marie heard the introduction as she stood at the desk where Lena sat.

"Remember," Lena announced, "the man who buys the girl's pie has the privilege of taking her home."

In an undertone, Marie said, "And that worries me. What if it's somebody you don't want to take you home? There are a couple of men here from Chestnut Flats. I don't like the way they look at me. I wouldn't want to be alone with them."

"Don't worry about it. The girl can choose a chaperone to ride along with them, if she wants to. If you have a questionable bidder, I'll follow you in my buggy, and if it's anyone that might cause trouble, I figure Daniel won't be far away. In the meantime, stand here beside me, forget your problems, listen to the sales, and try to learn the names and faces of the parents."

"Thanks," Marie said, and patted Lena on the shoulder. "The Lord was sure good to me when He allowed me to move into your home."

"That goes both ways, my dear."

Marie's throat tightened and she laid her hand on Lena's shoulder.

The pie sales started right away, and Marie enjoyed the good-natured rivalry of the men who delighted in trying to outbid their friends and neighbors. In her weaker moments, Marie had hoped that Daniel would buy her pie, and she'd considered dropping a hint as to which pie she'd made. Lena had told her it was a common practice for a man to find out from his girl what pie she'd made, but Marie didn't believe it would be a good example for the teacher to do so. Therefore, she said nothing, but she was ill at ease, wondering what the outcome of the evening would be. Although she wished Daniel would buy her pie, she didn't want to antagonize Viola, who wasn't above making a scene to humiliate anyone if she became offended.

As it turned out, however, there wasn't a problem because Viola devoted her attention to the visiting businessman, John Simpkins, who was interested in buying land in the Cove to start a furniture factory. The man was a business acquaintance of Viola's father, and he was spending the night at the Butler home. He must have persuaded Viola to tell him which pie she'd made, because he kept raising the bid.

Soon only the visitor and Daniel were bidding on her pie, and Viola was apparently delighted at the attention she was receiving. She sat on the edge of her chair, and her head turned back and forth from one bidder to the other as though her neck was on a pivot.

When the bid reached one hundred dollars, Daniel said, "That's all the money I brought tonight," and he bowed toward his competitor, "so I'll concede that Mr. Simpkins is the winner."

The crowd was disappointed when Daniel stopped. One man said, "Oh, come on, buddy, I'll loan you some money. I've still got fifty dollars left."

Daniel shook his head. "No, thank you. After all, Mr. Simpkins is a visitor in the Cove, and I don't want to spoil our reputation of fair treatment to visitors by taking all his money."

Laughing heartily, Simpkins said, "Don't let that stop you. There's plenty more where this came from."

Daniel shook his head, and the crowd must have known him well enough to realize he couldn't be persuaded, for they didn't argue further. Marie wondered if he would bid on her pie, but when one of the students started the bid on Marie's pie at ten cents, only a few people raised the bid, and the boy bought her pie for a quarter. Marie was grateful that the parents had been so considerate of her and the boy. She wanted to be an impartial teacher, treating all her pupils, and their parents, the same.

When they sat down to eat the pie, Marie invited the boy's parents and his two sisters to eat with them. "I'm sure your mother can bake a much better pie than I can," she said, trying to make them feel at ease with her, "but Mrs. Turner did help me make this one."

The two tiny girls sat on their mother's lap, staring wide-eyed at Marie and sucking their thumbs.

Jacob stood beside his father. Marie knew it was up to her to keep a conversation going, but she was as tongue-tied as the two girls. *I wish Mother was here. She'd know how to handle this situation.*

"I've made an effort to visit all the parents," Marie finally said, "but I haven't gotten to your home yet."

Clearing his throat, the man said, "You'd be welcome, but we live up on the mountain a ways. You'd have to walk, and it ain't a good idea to come by yourself. My name's Otho Burns, and my woman's name is Bertha."

"I'm glad to meet you," Marie said sincerely. She desperately wanted to reach the parents, as well as the children. "I like to walk, and I'm sure that Mrs. Turner will come with me. I'll try to visit you before too long. In the meantime, do you have any questions you'd like to ask me?"

The man shook his head. "No'm."

Marie had expected the evening to be endless, but time passed faster than she thought, and it didn't seem long until she stood by the door with Lena beside her, telling the audience goodbye. Almost everyone thanked her for hosting the pie supper, but because Lena and Lizzie had done almost all of the planning, she simply nodded her thanks and let it go at that.

When the crowd was gone, Marie sat at one of the desks and breathed deeply. "Well, I lived through my first hurdle as a teacher," she said. Looking at Lena, she said, "Did I make too many mistakes?"

Lena patted her on the shoulder. "No mistakes

at all. I'm sure everyone had a good time, and several told me they were happy you were going to be the teacher."

"Then I'll pray they still feel that way at the end of the school year."

Daniel blew out the lamps and locked the door before he brought Lena's buggy to the door and helped both the women into the vehicle.

"I'll get my horse and ride along with you," he said. "I'll rest better if I know you're home in bed asleep."

Marie said, "I'm not sure I'll be sleeping. I'm too tense to sleep, but I'm sure looking forward to relaxing on the feather mattress. I keep thinking of the people and all of the things they told me. This was a part of teaching I didn't know about."

"Well, you can rest assured that your first social activity with the students and their parents was successful," Daniel said. When they got to Lena's house, he told his grandmother, "You ladies go on inside. I'll put the buggy and horse in the barn and give the horse some hay. I hope you two will rest tonight."

He leaned over, kissed Lena on the cheek and squeezed Marie's hand as he helped them from the buggy.

Marie, too, had wished for a peaceful night's sleep, but her mind wouldn't rest. She kept thinking about the children and parents who'd attended, doubting that she was capable of ministering to these families. Their backgrounds were so different from the environment she'd always known. Feeling very childish, she started crying, wishing she was back home in Canaan in her own bed, knowing that her parents were nearby if she needed them.

To Marie, it seemed as if the weeks zipped by. When she returned to Canaan for Thanksgiving, she wasn't surprised to find that her mother had already been busy preparing candy and nut treats, as well as buying gifts to put under the Christmas tree. When Marie expressed her thanks, Evelyn said, "Lena told me it's customary for the teacher to buy gifts for all of the children, and then have sacks of candy, apples and oranges for everyone who attends the program. I know you could have managed without my help, but I wanted to do this."

"Now, Mother," Marie said, "I don't expect you and Dad to pay for that candy. The trustees are providing money for the treats."

"I know, but many people attend these programs, and I don't want you to be fretting that you won't have enough. Aunt Fannie and I will bake cookies and make fudge, so you'll have them in Canaan before you need them."

"No wonder people call me 'that spoiled Bolden brat.'"

Grinning, Evelyn said, "No one had better say that to Aunt Fannie, or they'll have a fight on their hands."

Laughing lightly, Marie said, "After the restrictions you and Aunt Fannie put on Earl and me when we were kids, I doubt that we'll stray too far from your teachings."

"I do worry about you, though, and want to see you safely married."

"I pray that I will get married and have a family someday, but you've done a good job of teaching that I should never be 'yoked together with an unbeliever.' Regardless of the way I feel, I absolutely have no intention of marrying anyone who doesn't share my faith. You have nothing to worry about."

"To the contrary," Evelyn said, "there's plenty to worry about. When I consider the love between Vance and me, I want very much for you to enjoy a similar relationship. Keep praying. God still answers prayers!"

Marie returned to Cades Cove refreshed from her visit home. She had no sooner removed the Thanksgiving decorations from the schoolroom until it was time to prepare a Christmas program. She learned from Lena that it was customary to have the program on the last day before the Christmas break.

Wanting to glean from her experience, she asked Lena's advice. "You need to involve all of the children," she said, "and speaking from experience, make it as simple as possible. After you've taught as many years as I have, you'll know that all parents want to see their children involved in some way."

"Mama gave me a program book she ordered from Raleigh. The scene takes place in Heaven the day before Jesus was born. All the participants are angels."

"That sounds as if it's the perfect drama for you. Everyone can be involved."

First, though, Marie had been warned by both her mother and Lena that there was usually a slump in children's attention prior to the Christmas break, and she tried to think of something interesting to be a teaching tool, and to occupy the minds of the children. She'd collected several books on the history of Cades Cove, and when she taught a few lessons on this history to the older students, she was amazed to find out how little many of them knew about the surrounding area. She decided that during the time between Thanksgiving and the Christmas break each student would be required to choose a hands-on project about the area to supplement the textbook lessons.

"The purpose of this assignment," she explained, "is to learn what it was like to live in this area fifty years ago. They lived closer to the land than we do now. Many of us who live in North Carolina today have made friends with the Native Americans, so I hope several of you will focus on the interaction of the natives and the early settlers. As you know, my brother, Earl, will be marrying a Cherokee. Our generation owes a big debt to these earlier settlers.

"The first Cades Cove pioneers, John and Lucretia Oliver, made a hundred-mile journey when they moved to this wilderness area in 1818. They could have run into a lot of danger, but the Cherokee were kind to them and shared their food with the Olivers during their first winter."

When two of her students, sisters Annabelle and

Norma Sandusky, asked her if they could prepare a paper on the life of Cherokee women, Marie was pleased with their choice. She monitored their work as they progressed and learned many interesting facts about the life of those early women. She was particularly interested in one description of that period of history, and Marie remembered that Lena had told her, "You'll learn a lot. The teachers always learn more than the students they teach."

As she helped the children research, Marie came across a statement that she wanted to remember, and she copied it in one of her teaching books. "Many Cherokee women adhered to the traditional belief that linked the spiritual and physical worlds into a balanced whole, emphasizing the importance of community and harmony. Those native women certainly had more prestige and power than other Colonial women in the area."

Although Marie thought that she might be expecting too much from her students, at the end of two weeks, she was pleasantly surprised at the projects they'd done. No doubt some of the parents had helped the students make toys handcrafted out of wood. One child brought a jar of molasses he'd helped his grandmother make. Jars of jelly were put on display. One of the older students made a replica of the John Oliver cabin, which had been built in 1822.

As she assessed the progress of the students during the few months she'd been with them, Marie knew she'd made many mistakes, but when she considered all that they had done, she knew she had proven to herself that she *could* teach.

Lena had warned her that the days between Thanksgiving and Christmas were the second most difficult time to be a teacher. "I suppose you can guess which time is the most difficult," Lena had said.

"Christmas, of course!" Marie said and her face spread into a wide smile. "Remember it hasn't been very long since I've been a 'pupil,' and I well recall that I could hardly stand the waiting time, at least the week before Christmas. Do you have any suggestions? I've participated in a lot of programs in my short life, but I've never planned one. I'm not too satisfied with my work so far."

As usual, Lena encouraged her. Placing her arms around Marie, she said, "You're one of the best teachers we've ever had in Cades Cove, so don't ever apologize for your work."

Fortified by Lena's praise, Marie took a deep breath. "With that kind of praise, I'd better not disappoint you. My mother gave me a program book. We'll start practicing on the program the first of the week. I'll have the students study in the morning and then work on the program in the afternoon." After a few weeks of rehearsals Marie was satisfied with the children's progress.

Lena had told her that it was customary to trim a tree and that the teacher gave sacks of candy, as well as an apple or orange to *everyone,* not just the students. As usual, she relied on Lena for advice about what the students and parents would expect for the holidays.

"I figure if you dig deep enough, you'll find that there's a box of Christmas ornaments to decorate a tree."

"Oh, my," Marie wailed. "Why didn't they mention all of these things in teachers college?"

Laughing, Lena said, "Probably because they figured if prospective teachers had any idea of the hard work it takes to be a teacher, they wouldn't have many graduates."

"There isn't any problem about having the treats. I brought the candy and fruit back with me after Thanksgiving vacation. It's been in my bedroom, so that will be ready."

Lena told Marie, "Perhaps you don't realize it, but the Christmas program is the highlight of the year for most of the children, and certainly for the parents, who seldom have an opportunity to leave the Cove."

When the day of the Christmas program finally arrived, Marie felt that it was going to be a success. Although the rehearsal sessions had sometimes turned into disasters, with students forgetting their speeches and some bursting into tears because they'd made a mistake, Marie was more than pleased with the program.

Every participant was an angel, and several women had worked after school hours for a few days making garments for them to wear. Everyone was wrapped in a white sheet, and each child wore a halo made by tying the ends from pine branches around their foreheads. Although during rehearsal, the children had complained about the pine needles scratching their heads, their behavior was very angel-like on the night of the program.

Marie had high hopes for the success of the program. The evening started with the audience singing Christmas carols with the children. Obviously, the children enjoyed all of the Christmas carols, but they seemed to prefer Martin Luther's Cradle Hymn, as did the audience, who sang joyfully, "Away in a manger, no crib for a bed…"

The program progressed without too many mistakes and no real disasters, and parents and children alike enjoyed the festive celebration of the Christmas season.

With the help of Lena and Lizzie, Marie had filled brown bags with candy and nuts. Adults, as well as the children, received a gift from under the tall cedar that stood in one corner of the room.

When it was over, Marie was satisfied that though it hadn't been a perfect school year so far, she'd done the best that she could.

After the audience left, Daniel stayed behind to help straighten the room, so that it would be ready for classes after the Christmas break.

When he'd helped his grandmother into the buggy, he went back to lock the schoolhouse door.

As Marie stepped outside, he said, "Have you

made arrangements to return to Canaan? If not, I'll be glad to take you."

"Thank you," Marie said, not knowing whether she was pleased that Daniel had asked, or sorry that she couldn't accept his offer. "I appreciate that, but Dad sent word that he would be here early tomorrow morning to take me home."

"I hope you have a good visit at home." He reached into his pocket and removed a small box. "Merry Christmas," he said.

"Oh," Marie said, "you shouldn't have given me a gift."

"Why not?" he said and she sensed that he was displeased. "I didn't make the money bootlegging."

"I didn't even think of such a thing."

"Then will you take the gift?"

She took the box, then stood on tiptoes and kissed his cheek. Wondering why on earth she'd done such a thing, she was rather amused when she realized that Daniel was as startled as she was. "Merry Christmas," she said, and ran down the steps and got into Lena's buggy. If Lena had noticed the kiss, she didn't mention it.

At times, Marie had thought that Daniel didn't even like her, and she was taken completely by surprise when he'd handed her the gift. Although she was curious about the present, she didn't open it until Christmas morning. She'd not mentioned the gift to her parents.

Although she didn't know anything about pearls, she was sure that the black Tahitian pearls were expensive, which wasn't surprising. For some reason, Marie started crying, and she didn't know why—no doubt because her future with Daniel seemed to be as dark as the beautiful pearls she clasped around her neck.

Chapter 6

Although Marie thoroughly enjoyed the days at home with her family during Christmas break, her mind didn't stray far from Cades Cove and the friends she'd made there. Aunt Fannie prepared all of Marie's favorite dishes and coddled her as if she was a child again. She visited her friends in town, and spent one afternoon in the little church where the Canaanites worshipped. Attending services in this building was one of her earliest memories.

The wooden pulpit still stood on the platform in the front of the building. Two rows of six benches faced the front. An organ was placed to the left of the pulpit, and two armchairs were on the right. There was still a faint odor of the cedar logs used to erect the building. She remembered vividly the morning she'd gone forward when the pastor gave the invitation to those who wanted to be saved and follow the Lord in baptism. She shivered when she also recalled how cold the water was when she was baptized.

A Bible lay face open on the podium, and curious, she looked to see what portion of the Scripture had been used the previous Sunday. She remembered that one of their pastors had involved the children in the worship service by asking them to memorize certain Scripture verses. One Sunday, he'd said, "When you have Bible verses stored in your mind and heart, they can never be taken away from you." To encourage them to read and memorize, one summer he'd asked the children under the age of twelve to repeat any Bible verse they had learned during that particular week.

Marie laughed when she remembered how many children had quoted, "Jesus wept."

However, their pastor never took lightly the effort any child made.

Reverently, Marie turned the pages of the book, asking God to direct her to a portion of Scripture that would give her some insight on how to deal with her relationship with Daniel. Weeks ago she had memorized a passage from Paul's second message to the Corinthians—a message that seemed seared in her memory.

"Be ye not unequally yoked together with unbelievers—for what fellowship hath righteousness with unrighteousness? And what communion hath light with darkness."

Kneeling beside the pulpit, Marie prayed, "God, our Father, what am I to do? I love Daniel, and I have a feeling that he's under conviction and knows he needs to follow You. I don't know how to pray, except to depend on You to make him see the error of his ways. He knows what he *should* do, but he's proud and believes that he doesn't *need* anyone. Will You pierce his hardened heart and direct his thoughts toward You?"

Marie stood, gave another fond look around the room where she'd accepted God as the supreme leader in her life. She felt comforted and assured that somehow, some way, Daniel would be convinced of his need to change his ways.

As she walked back to Sunrise Manor, she realized that Canaan hadn't changed much. She also admitted that it was no longer the most important place in her life, but rather a pleasant memory of the past. She'd cast her lot temporarily with Cades Cove, but she wondered how long she would live there. It seemed almost like home to her. She'd enjoyed visiting with her family, but she looked forward to returning to her teaching job, even though she had several problems to deal with when she returned.

How was she ever going to teach Guy Alexander to read? Would Janie Moss always have the sniffles? How should she deal with the advances of Bill Frazier who, at least once a week, stopped by the schoolhouse to discuss how his daughter Olive was progressing in school? So far, he hadn't given her any cause to believe that he hadn't made these visits solely in the interest of his daughter. Still, she was uneasy in his presence, and one of the reasons she didn't trust him was the sly expression on his face when she looked his way unexpectedly. She considered talking to Daniel about her reservations, but if he should say anything to Frazier, it might disrupt her teaching. She was very fond of Olive, and feared if she mentioned the situation to anyone it might cause the student some trouble, so she suffered in silence.

Also, she hadn't yet found the time to walk up the mountain to where Smith Spencer lived, and she wanted to do that as soon as possible.

Vance was prepared to take Marie back to Cades Cove when her Christmas vacation was over. On the day before her return, a knock sounded on the door. Marie and her mother were in the living room, so Aunt Fannie padded down the hallway to greet the visitor.

They heard the door open, and suddenly Aunt Fannie shouted, "Well, the Lawd be praised! Glory! Glory! You rascal, come in here and let me give you a hug."

Marie and Evelyn looked at one another, stood up quickly and headed toward the door.

Marie had never been so surprised in her life. Earl stood in the hallway, with Awinta by his side. Both of them looked somewhat uneasy, probably wondering what kind of reception they would get. Vance had been in his office, but he hurried into the hallway.

Earl looked as if he wasn't sure of his welcome, but he said, "Mother, Dad, I want you to meet my friend, Awinta."

Instead of having on her native garments, Awinta was dressed in a dark red coat, which Marie thought was probably a recent purchase. Her long black hair hung over her shoulders, and golden earrings graced her earlobes. She was so beautiful that tears formed in Marie's eyes.

Evelyn made the first move toward them, but Vance wasn't far behind. They both threw their arms around their hermit son, and then Evelyn pulled Awinta into the circle.

"Oh, son," Vance said, "I'm so glad to see you. And is this young lady your wife?"

Tears were glistening in Earl's eyes. "Not yet! We came to get permission from you and Mother."

Trying to frown, but smiling instead, Vance said, "And what will you do if we refuse permission?"

"She won't marry me if you won't give your permission," Earl admitted. "That's why we're here."

After Aunt Fannie gave Earl a strong hug, she turned to Awinta and held her at arms' length. "Now, you be good to my boy," she admonished.

"I intend to," Awinta said, smiling. "I love him very much."

The family moved into the parlor and spent the next hour catching up and talking over the wedding plans.

A knock sounded at the door, and Aunt Fannie hustled down the hallway once again.

They heard a masculine voice, and Aunt Fannie answered, "Yes, sir, come right in. Missy Evelyn and Marie are in the parlor. This way, please."

Marie's heartbeat quickened. The voice sounded like Daniel's, but could it be? Evelyn stood and went to the parlor door.

"Company, missus," Aunt Fannie said.

"I hope I'm not intruding, Mrs. Bolden," the masculine voice said. Marie gasped, wondering why Daniel was in Canaan. She'd know that voice anywhere.

"I'm Daniel Watson, Lena Turner's grandson. I came to Canaan yesterday to take care of some business, and my grandmother suggested that it might be convenient for me to bring Marie back to Cade's Cove when I return home tomorrow."

"Come in, Mr. Watson," Evelyn said. "That was thoughtful of your grandmother."

Evelyn led Daniel into the parlor and introduced him first to Vance. Daniel shook Vance's hand, and when Evelyn turned to introduce him to Earl and Awinta, he said, "We met in Cades Cove, Mrs. Bolden." Addressing the family at large he added, "I didn't mean to intrude on your family time. I should be going."

Evelyn said, "Nonsense. Please join us," and indicated an empty chair beside Marie.

Marie had stood when Daniel entered the room, and now she sat down. She'd heard what Daniel said in the hall, and while everyone talked around her, her mind was on the next day. She both anticipated and dreaded taking the long drive between Canaan and Cades Cove with only Daniel for company. However, the physical and emotional attractions between them were strong enough that she felt they had to deal with the situation. Too many things separated her and Daniel, and perhaps the long drive would be a good time to discuss the difficulties of a relationship between them.

She turned to Daniel and said, "Earlier today we were saying that Dad probably shouldn't go out tomorrow. He's had a bad cough for a few days, and we don't think he's in any physical condition to take the round-trip between Canaan and Cades Cove. Jasper, who works for Dad, was planning to drive me to the Cove, but it will save him a trip if I go with you. What time do you plan to leave?"

"Will midmorning be convenient for you?"

"Yes, of course."

Aunt Fannie entered the room with a tray.

"Here's coffee, tea and cookies, missus. Anything else you need?"

"No, thank you, Fannie. I'll serve our guests. Will you be staying for dinner, Mr. Watson?"

"No, thank you. I'm visiting at the home of my cousin, who lives here in Canaan. I'll be eating there."

Marie's pulse accelerated as she listened to them talk, and she was glad that her mother took the initiative in visiting with Daniel while Vance talked with Earl and Awinta. Marie seemed to be tongue-tied, and when she did make a comment, it didn't amount to much.

When he finished drinking a cup of coffee, Daniel stood up. "I still have some items to purchase here in Canaan, so I'll be leaving." Turning to Marie, he said, "Shall I meet you here tomorrow morning at ten o'clock?"

"That's convenient for me. And I'm sure Aunt Fannie will have a big basket of food for us to take."

Daniel took his leave of the rest of the family and departed. Marie walked him to the front porch and watched as he mounted his horse and rode down the street.

Later in the evening while Vance continued to visit with Earl and Awinta in the parlor and Aunt Fannie took her keen ears down the hallway to the kitchen, Evelyn said, "I'm impressed with Daniel. He seems like a fine man, but you don't seem to be sure about him."

Marie went to sit beside her mother, and Evelyn put a comforting arm around her. "Well, yes and no," Marie said honestly.

"I'll listen if you want to talk about it."

"I've wanted to talk to you for weeks. I sensed an immediate emotional and physical attraction to Daniel the first time we met, and it hasn't gone away. And from the dazed expression on his face at our first meeting, I believe he experienced the same feelings that I did. He hasn't made any strong overtures, and

I don't see him often, but he's in my mind so much of the time that it upsets me."

She reached inside her pocket for the pearls he'd recently given her. "He gave these to me before I left the Cove, and I didn't open the gift until Christmas morning. I want to keep them, but I don't suppose you'd approve. I've always thought that falling in love would be a wonderful experience, so why am I so miserable?"

Smiling, Evelyn said, "True love often has its ups and downs. I speak from experience, as you know. I won't tell you what to do. I have no doubt that you'll make the right decision."

"I love him," Marie said. "However, I don't want you to worry, for I won't let my feelings overcome my common sense. Daniel isn't the kind of man I'd want to marry, at least I don't think so right now, so I'm not planning to follow my heart. His grandmother knows how I feel, and we've prayed often about a solution to the situation, but we haven't gotten an answer about what is best for both of us. Fortunately, I'm so busy with my school teaching that I don't see him often."

"You know that since you reached the age of twenty I haven't meddled in your life, or Earl's, either," Evelyn said. "I figured that if your father and I hadn't taught you right from wrong by that time, it was too late to start. But I will ask this—what's wrong with Daniel Watson that would make him objectionable as your friend, and even more than that, if my eyes don't deceive me?"

"Well, for one thing, he isn't a believer, and you taught Earl and me from our early teens that we shouldn't be 'yoked' together with nonbelievers."

Nodding, Evelyn said, "And I still believe that *is* the right way, but I know of a few mixed marriages, where the nonbeliever does accept our Christian faith. Is there any hope that Daniel could be converted to our beliefs and way of life?"

"None that I've detected. Besides, if I should marry now, there aren't many school trustees who will hire a married woman as their schoolteacher, and I'd want to continue teaching even if I did marry. I've heard the saying 'a woman's place is in the home' so many times that I feel like screaming when someone mentions it in my presence. I just don't see why a married woman can't have a career just like a married man."

Laughing, Evelyn put her arm around Marie's waist and kissed her on the cheek. "I encountered the same biases years ago when I became a missionary. I understand what you're experiencing."

"I figure Dad twisted a lot of arms, or I wouldn't have been hired to teach in Cades Cove in the first place. So do I follow my heart or my teaching profession?"

Evelyn shook her head. "I don't have an answer for you, my dear, but if it's God's will that Daniel Watson is the man for you, He will provide a way."

Sighing deeply, Marie stood, saying, "I must get ready so I won't keep Daniel waiting in the morning."

She stopped at the foot of the stairs and said, "Life will always have blessings and disappointments, I suppose. Which reminds me, I'm so glad you and Father are coming to Earl's wedding."

"We'll be there if I have to drag your father, though I don't think I'll have to. I've prayed that Earl would finally settle down, and I think Awinta is a good match for him. I wouldn't miss being there to wish them well. I wish he would come to Canaan to be married, though, because I know Aunt Fannie would like to attend the wedding and it would be so beautiful here."

"I know. But all of Awinta's family is there. It would be harder for all of them to come here than for you to go there."

"I didn't think of it that way, but of course you're right."

"I was afraid Papa would be unhappy to have a native girl for his daughter-in-law, but he seems to be quite taken with Awinta."

"He does seem to like her very much, doesn't he? A few years ago, he would have been upset, but time has mellowed him. We've made several good Cherokee friends over the years, so he'll accept Awinta into the family."

That night, Marie's dreams were troubled by far-fetched visions of Daniel clinging to a tree that overlooked a large precipice. Another dream showed a preacher marrying a couple, but the bride and groom had their backs to her, surrounded by a wisp of fog. Was that Earl and his bride? It looked more like Daniel and her. She was awakened by a rapid heartbeat, wondering why she was so troubled. She couldn't go back to sleep, so she slipped out of bed and prepared to return to Cades Cove.

Daniel was at the door at the time he'd indicated he would call for her. Vance left his room to give her a hug before she left, although he omitted the kiss on the cheek that he usually gave her because he didn't want her to catch his ailment.

Obviously concerned over Marie's unease, Evelyn whispered in her ear, "God can make all things right. I'll be praying."

"Please do. I want to make the right decision for everyone concerned."

Daniel and Vance discussed the weather, noting that there were a few clouds in the sky. "I hope you don't run into any showers before you get home," Vance said.

"I have a cover for the buggy if that happens," Daniel said, and motioning to the boxes behind the seat, he added, "I have a tarpaulin with me, if I have to cover them."

"Is there room for this basket?" Evelyn queried. "Aunt Fanny and I packed some sandwiches and fruit for you."

Laughing, Daniel said, "I can always make room for food." He took Marie's arm and helped her into the buggy, then stored the lunch under the seat.

"Don't forget to write," Evelyn said, as Daniel picked up the reins, lightly touched the pinto's haunches and they headed out of town. He handled the horse carefully and expertly, and Marie wondered if there was anything he couldn't do.

They were quiet for the first mile or two, and Marie racked her brain to think of a subject that wouldn't plunge them into an argument. She observed the small stream they were following and the scattered white clouds.

"This is turning out to be a beautiful day," she said.

He agreed and they continued to talk about mundane things, until Daniel finally said, "Well, are we going to ride all the way to Cades Cove without discussing the important things?"

"Such as?"

"This overwhelming attraction between us! And don't tell me you don't feel it, too. I'm as aware of you as if I've known you all of my life. Something happened to me the first day I saw you—a feeling I'd never had before. I'd heard of love at first sight, but I didn't believe there was such a thing. I do now. How about you?"

Marie supposed she could pretend she didn't know what he was talking about, but instead, she said, "Yes, I'm aware of it, but I don't believe we should even bother to discuss the situation. I can't see any future for us. It would have been better if we'd never met. Our lifestyles are too different."

"What do you mean?"

"I don't believe everything I hear," Marie said, not looking at him, "and I don't invite gossip, but if your private life is like I've heard, we don't have much in common. For one thing, my parents have tried to guide my choices in life, and one of the main things I've known as long as I can remember is that we shouldn't be unequally yoked together in the spiritual sense. In other words, I shouldn't marry anyone who doesn't share my spiritual beliefs."

"My lifestyle is probably not as bad as you've heard," Daniel said, and his brilliant eyes glistened ominously. "I don't care what people think. If someone tells a lie about me, I figure it can't hurt as long as it isn't the truth. So I just go my merry way."

"That's your privilege, but not the kind of example I'd want my children to see every day. And I *do* mind when people say false things about me."

"Why?"

"For one thing, any gossip about me is a reflection on my parents, indicating they didn't train me as they should have. Also, it upsets me when my reputation is tarnished without cause. There's a Scripture verse from the writings of Timothy that I repeat often. 'Let no man despise thy youth; but be thou an example of the believers, in word, in conversation, in charity, in spirit, in faith, in purity.'"

"Don't spout Scripture at me. I get enough of that from Granny."

The more they talked, the angrier Marie became, and she knew by the terse, scornful expression on Daniel's face that he was angry, too. Fortunately, she could see the rooftops of Canaan in the distance, and she was relieved they didn't have much farther to go.

She was tempted to get out of the buggy and walk the rest of the way, but she thought of Lena and she kept silent. However, when he stopped the horses in front of his grandmother's house, she jumped out of the buggy without his assistance. She didn't want Daniel to touch her.

"I apologize for 'preaching' to you," Marie said. "The Bible is so much a part of my life that it's natural for me to talk in terms of biblical ideals. I didn't realize I would offend you. I was happy to receive this appointment to Cades Cove because I've dreamed of being a teacher since I was a child, and I've received a lot of support from the trustees, but if you and I are going to quarrel back and forth for the rest of the year, I may have made a mistake."

Mad at herself because she'd overreacted to Daniel's comments, she snatched her suitcase from the back of the buggy and ran into the house. The house seemed empty and she went into her room, dropped her suitcase on the floor and lay on the bed. She half expected Daniel to follow her, but when she heard the horses speeding away, she realized that it was impossible for them to be friends, and certainly not more than friends. She didn't know whether to laugh or cry, and decided to have a good cry. She was still lying on the bed when she heard Lena's buggy arrive, and a short time later, she heard Lena come into the kitchen. When Lena knocked on Marie's door an hour later and said that supper was ready, Marie said, "I'm not hungry."

Daniel was the pride of Lena's life, and although

she knew Daniel's faults, he was her beloved grandson. But as angry as she was at Daniel, Marie knew
she couldn't hide her feelings from his grandmother.

Without an invitation, Lena opened the door and
came into the room and sat on the side of the bed.
"Well, it's obvious that you and Daniel have had a
fight. He nearly forced me off the road with his reck-
less driving, and you look as if you've been crying
because you've lost your last friend. If you want me
to mind my own business, tell me so and I'll leave
you alone."

Wanting nothing more than to leave Cades Cove,
Marie was determined that she wouldn't criticize
Daniel to his grandmother. "He's no more at fault
than I am. Not that he's ever asked me to marry him,
but if he should, and even if my parents approved, I
wouldn't consider marrying a man who doesn't share
my spiritual beliefs and practices. Daniel doesn't,
and he made it plain that he doesn't intend to change.
I think it will be better if I find another place to live."

Sighing, Lena said, "You and Daniel are a lot
alike, and I'm not the one to advise you, but why not
stay on here? You and I are friends now, and Daniel
can come visit me while you're at the schoolhouse.
I'll admit that I've been hoping you would become
my granddaughter, but I doubt that will ever happen.
However, both of you are angry now, and I'd advise
you not to make any hasty decisions about moving
away from my home for a few days. You won't find
many places in the Cove where you'd want to live."

"I don't want to leave you," Marie said, "and my

mother wouldn't approve of it, either. I can't avoid seeing Daniel the rest of the year, so I'll make an effort to watch my temper. I've never had such a nasty temper before, but I've never been in love with anyone else, either. Pray for me that I'll be able to finish the rest of the year without making a lot of mistakes."

Chapter 7

Marie had been told when she moved to the Cove that sometimes the weather was so inclement during midwinter that school would often be dismissed for several days—days that had to be made up at the end of the school term. She was pleased when the weather was moderate enough that school had to be dismissed for only two days. Although she was busy all the time, Marie missed her parents. When she had only Saturdays and Sundays free, Marie didn't feel that it was good to make a lot of trips to Canaan. She didn't know what she would have done without the weekly letters she sent and exchanged with her mother.

A few weeks passed and Marie didn't see Daniel, but one Saturday she was involved in her weekly ironing while Lena sat in a nearby rocking chair, peeling potatoes. At her insistence, Marie had finally agreed to let Lena wash her garments, but she absolutely refused to let her iron them, as well. It was hot in the kitchen, and Marie felt the sweat running down her back.

"Do you know that you've probably lost ten pounds since you moved here?" Lena said. "You're working yourself to death. Your mother will think I haven't been feeding you enough."

Forcing a smile, Marie said, "I'm all right."

"I know as well as anyone that you want to do a good job, but why don't you rest occasionally? For the most part, residents of Cades Cove don't work themselves to death. We think that if we don't get all the work completed today, it will still be here tomorrow."

"I don't mind working, and I have to keep my mind occupied."

Lena didn't ask any questions. Marie knew that her landlady understood why Daniel had stopped coming to her home when Marie was there.

Marie had resigned herself to the belief that Daniel would continue avoiding her until the end of the term, so she was surprised two weeks later when he was at Lena's home when she returned home from school. He came out of the back door and walked down the steps to where she was dismounting.

"I have to go home now to help my farrier shoe some horses," he said, as if they'd parted on good terms at their last meeting, "but I'll stable the horse for you before I leave."

"Thanks," she said, lifting the saddlebags from the horse's rump. "I was playing hide-and-seek with the little kids today and they hid in some difficult places, so I'm very tired."

"Since tomorrow is Saturday, and the weather seems promising, it might be a good day for us to go visit Smith Spencer."

"Oh, you mean the hermit, as some of my students call him. Although they call Earl a hermit, too."

"Yes. Mr. Spencer is a hermit. But he's always willing to welcome visitors and you really haven't gotten a good idea of the Cove until you've met Smith."

"I'd like to visit with him. What time do you want to go?"

"I'll come by right after noon and pick you up in the buggy, but we'll have to do some climbing to get to his house, so you'll want to wear sturdy walking shoes."

He mounted his horse, waved goodbye and headed toward his home, with his horse cantering along the road.

While they were eating supper, Lena said, "Didn't I hear you making plans to walk up the mountain with Daniel tomorrow afternoon?"

Marie nodded, and smiled. "Yes—I'm really eager to meet Mr. Spencer."

"Well, although you'll have some rough terrain to ride along and the last part is a steep climb on foot,

I'll admit it is worth the trip. He's the oldest living resident of the early pioneers to the Cove. I've heard one of the early pioneers said that his ancestors survived their first winter here only because the Cherokee provided food for them. Smith will probably tell you all about that."

The next afternoon, Marie sat and listened in awe as the aged man talked about his ancestors and how they survived their first winter in the mountains because the Native Americans *had* provided food for them. The man believed that the hand of God was responsible for the survival of the early settlers. The pioneering families built several church buildings, as well as dwellings.

"Were the houses made of logs?" Marie questioned.

"Many of them were, but were later modernized with frame construction. The community grew and prospered, but their mutual faith survived the first harsh winter. Very few children left the Cove—they lived to manhood and womanhood here. The community grew and prospered, and the children matured to establish later generations of Cades Cove's families. Quite a few had the wanderlust and moved westward, but a large number remained and lived the rest of their lives right here in the Cove."

"Were you born here?"

"No, but my parents were. I was only a child when we moved. I remember them talking about the first settlers, John and Lucretia Oliver, who traveled over a hundred miles to move to Cades Cove. The Olivers were poor when they moved to the Cove, and there wasn't a settlement of any kind, but they brought seed and a few tools with them. There was also the danger that the Cherokee would be hostile, but all turned out well. The pioneers were busy clearing the land and building their cabin, and they didn't have time to plant enough crops to keep them through the winter. If it hadn't been for the Cherokee, who shared their food with them, the Oliver family would have starved."

"What else can you tell me about the early settlers in Cades Cove?" Marie asked. "Sometimes, I feel very unlearned when some of my students know more about the history of this country than I do."

Daniel sat in a chair that was obviously made by hand. She had already learned that Mr. Spencer gave a lot of thought to what he wanted to say before he opened his mouth, and when he leaned back in his rocking chair and closed his eyes, Marie wondered if he was thinking or if he'd gone to sleep. Judging from his dark features, she'd decided that Mr. Spencer had some Cherokee blood in him.

Daniel winked at her, yawned and twiddled his thumbs, so instead of asking any questions, she remained silent, looking around the interesting cabin. Several deer heads and antlers decorated the wall. A cured black bearskin was spread across a davenport that had seen better days. A slight fire burned in the large fireplace that spread across almost one whole wall of the cabin. It was very warm in the cabin, and

Marie had gotten drowsy when Mr. Spencer stirred and started talking, still with his eyes shut.

"The Cherokee have been in this part of Tennessee for almost two hundred years. They had established a village here, which was known as Otter Place. The village was nothing more than a hunting camp along the flat land of Cove Creek. An early explorer by the name of Timberlake reported that the creeks and rivers in this area were full of otters, but they were gone by the time the first Europeans settled here."

"When I was a kid," Daniel said, "I often wished that I could have been living here during that time, but I understand that living conditions weren't comfortable in the early days. Didn't you tell me once that the Cherokee left when the Europeans settled in Cades Cove?"

Spencer nodded his head. "The explorers and early settlers didn't treat the Cherokee right. By the 1820s the Cherokee lost all claim to this part of Tennessee, then when Andrew Jackson was the president, he made the natives move westward, some to the Southern states, others into Oklahoma. The ancestors of the present Cherokee in this area hid in the mountains from Jackson's soldiers, and became the ancestors of the natives here today."

Spencer looked toward Marie, saying, "Is that all you need to know, missy, or do you have other questions?"

"Just about the effect the War Between the States had on the Cherokee. My dad fought in the Confederate army and, although he doesn't talk much about his experiences, he did mention that the Confederates raided Cades Cove several times during the latter part of the Civil War. Do you know anything about that?"

Spencer nodded. "There weren't any big battles, but lots of skirmishes between the Federals and Confederates around this area. Matter of fact, Cades Cove dwellers suffered from the effects of the war as well as the Confederate states along the Atlantic." Shaking his head, Spencer said, "War's a terrible thing, missy."

Up to this point Marie had assumed that Mr. Spencer was a sober man without a humorous side to his personality, so she was surprised when he erupted into a loud guffaw. Apparently some memory amused him.

"I've told you about the bad times in the Cove, but the early settlers had a good time and enjoyed life. Of course, people didn't live as long then. There wasn't much medicine, so the average life span of the settlers was forty-five years."

"I've heard Granny say that most people married as teenagers," Daniel commented.

"That's a fact," Spencer said. "Youngsters started courtin' as early as thirteen or fourteen years old."

"Yes, Granny tells me often," Daniel said, "that girls who didn't get married by the time they turned eighteen or twenty were considered 'old maids.' She brings that subject up often to me for she thinks I should have married years ago, though maybe men aren't expected to marry so early."

Spencer nodded his head, and cast an amused glance in Marie's direction, and she felt herself blushing, thankful that the room was so dark that no one could see her red face.

"Your Granny is right about that, son. It's high time you married and started a family. But let me finish about the early settlers. The people used most any kind of work to have a good time. They had lots of church meetings and picnics where they celebrated, and they even made work sound like fun."

"Yeah, I've heard about their chestnut harvests, corn husking and molasses making. They even made a competition of stringing beans."

"The early settlers did lots of hard work, but we enjoyed ourselves, too," Spencer commented.

Marie didn't want to wear her welcome out, so she said, "I really appreciate hearing your comments about a period of history that has influenced the lives of so many people, both for bad and good. Although my father fought for the Confederacy without any serious physical injuries, he still bears inward scars that he'll carry to his grave."

When she stood, Daniel got up from his chair and shook hands with their host.

"Come again, both of you," Spencer said. "I'm alone most of the time with only my memories to keep me company."

The visit with this aged man had been not only informational, but also such a pleasure, and at his insistence, Marie promised him that she would visit again.

It was more difficult to descend the mountainside than it had been to climb it, so Daniel held Marie's hand most of the way.

"Thanks very much," she said to Daniel, "for going with me to see Mr. Spencer. As soon as I get home, I intend to record everything he told us. I took some notes, but I'd get so interested in what he was saying that I'd forget to make any record."

"Granny and I can probably fill in some of the information if you missed anything."

As they walked companionably down the mountainside toward where the buggy was parked, Daniel said, "Sometimes I do wish I could have lived in an earlier period. I believe I would have enjoyed being a pioneer, rather than to have inherited a farm that doesn't require a lot of work. Everything I have was given to me, so I don't suppose I'll ever know if I would have liked being an early settler."

Marie didn't comment, although she believed that no matter what Daniel tried, he would succeed at the task. They walked a large part of the trail in silence, and Marie again sensed the comradeship between them. Her mother had always said that there was a difference between being in love and companionship, and she'd urged her children to be sure that they enjoyed both attributes with the person they married. What did she feel toward Daniel? It wasn't a question she could answer, although she feared her future was bound to this man.

* * *

Constantly concerned that she was responsible for the education of her students, and knowing that she was a novice in that position, Marie dreaded hearing the evaluation the school trustees would give her, and the morning they made their surprise annual visit was a burden to her. When they entered the building, she greeted them, praying that the students would be able to answer questions they asked. The three men spent most of the morning listening to the lessons Marie had prepared, and she was gratified when they gave her a good report. She had no doubt that she would be asked to teach again the following year, but she was relieved that she didn't have to make a decision right away.

Although Earl was busy with trapping throughout the winter, he still stopped by the schoolhouse to see Marie periodically. On one of his visits he told Marie that he and Awinta had finally set the date for their wedding: the first week in June. The last day of school was May 20. Rather than return to Canaan and come back again, Marie told her parents that she'd wait until after the wedding and then go back to Canaan with them, rather than have her father make an extra trip.

As it turned out, Marie was glad that she *had* planned to stay on because after the last day of school, she needed several extra days to store all of the equipment and books. She was also expected, Lena informed her, to give the building a thorough cleaning. Remembering the cleaning they'd given the schoolhouse prior to starting the school session in the autumn, Marie didn't see any reason to do a thorough cleaning, and she expressed her opinion to Lena.

"I'll work alongside of you, of course, and some of the other women will also help," Lena explained. "Still, it takes a couple of days to have the place in good enough shape to suit the trustees. They're rather fussy at times but, of course," she added with a laugh, "that's why we elect them."

Although she loved her family and enjoyed being with them, Marie wasn't looking forward to the summer vacation as much as she should be, and she knew why. Daniel had been gone on a business trip to Charleston, South Carolina, through part of the winter, and she had missed seeing him during the visits he made to Lena's home. Although she was pretty sure there wasn't any future for her and Daniel, she kept thinking about what might have been. She'd grown accustomed to seeing Daniel now and then, and it was upsetting that she wouldn't be seeing him during the summer months.

She'd already been approached by the school trustees to return the next fall, which was gratifying, but she'd asked for another few days to make her decision.

The invitation indicated that her record was good enough or she wouldn't have been offered a second term. She wanted to return to Cades Cove, but was it a good idea to keep punishing herself by seeing Daniel when she knew they could never have a life together?

* * *

One evening near the close of school, when she left the building, Daniel was sitting on the steps. He scooted over and made room for her to sit beside him.

"I'm going to miss you this summer," he said. She set the basket she carried on the ground and sat beside him.

"It's good to be missed, but I am tired. I suppose it's been a good year, but I can think of lots of things I should have done better."

"I've not heard any complaints about your teaching. The children all seem to like you and several parents have told me they're glad you're returning. So am I."

Marie didn't know where this conversation was heading, but she told him she hadn't decided yet whether to return.

"Will your parents object if I come to see you this summer?"

"I doubt it. They've pretty much allowed Earl and me to make our own decisions."

"Then would you welcome me if I came to see you?"

"I don't know," she said honestly. "It might help if you answer some questions."

Frowning, he said, "Such as?"

"Do you operate a still? Do you sell moonshine?"

His face turned red, and Marie could tell that he was angry. "No, I don't!"

"Then why do you let the local citizens believe that you do?"

"It's nobody's business what I do."

"It would be *mine* if we ever become more than friends."

"We're already more than friends, and you know it! What's the next question?"

"I've heard talk around town that Viola Butler spent the night at your house several weeks ago. Did she?"

"Yes, she did! But you shouldn't listen to gossip because you don't know what really happened."

Standing and picking up her basket, she said, "You've told me all I need to know. You've answered the question as to why you aren't welcome to court me. In addition to those two things, my parents have always taught me that believers should not marry nonbelievers. I believe that, and as far as I'm concerned, that means not to keep company with them, either. I'll be honest with you and say that I'd like very much for us to be more than friends but, Daniel, there are too many differences in our lifestyles. When two people marry, they have to realize that they can't go their separate ways anymore. In the wedding service, there's a phrase that says, 'the two shall become one.' I believe that's the only way to have a happy marriage."

"I didn't expect to get another sermon," he said. "Besides, I haven't asked you to marry me."

It wasn't the words he said, but the anger in his voice that hurt Marie's feelings. His eyes glittered angrily, too. Tears filled her eyes as she started toward the shed where her horse waited. Although it was too late for her to not fall in love with Daniel, at least she'd seen the worst side of him in time to prevent her from marrying him; that is, if he even had marriage in mind.

Marie didn't think it was possible for her to feel any worse, but when she arrived at the Turner home and saw Viola sitting on the porch swing with Lena, she felt like screaming. And Viola's greeting didn't help lighten her mood.

"Well, here's the weary schoolmarm, home after a hard day's work. Honey, I don't know what you're trying to prove, but why don't you admit that you've had enough, go home and forget about Cades Cove?"

Instead of answering, Marie opened the door and went into the house, with Viola's sarcastic laughter following her. Throughout the school year, Viola had seemed to make a point of irritating her by commenting about the relationship she enjoyed with Daniel. Lena insisted to Marie that Viola was jealous of her. According to Lena, the relationship was a figment of Viola's imagination. Daniel had never been serious in his attention to Viola; Viola was the pursuer and Daniel, being a gentleman, didn't rebuff her completely. Marie admitted that could be true, but she also realized that Lena, as could be expected, could find little fault in her grandson. Although her sojourn in Cades Cove had been extremely rewarding, there were times when Marie wished she'd never heard of the place.

She sat on the side of the bed, wondering if she

should agree to teach at Cades Cove the following school year. The thing that bothered her most was the possibility that her attitude had turned Daniel even farther from God. If she saw him more often, perhaps she could set the right example before him, thus encouraging him toward a better way of life.

But she couldn't spend more time with him if the gossip was correct. John Simpkins had returned to his home in Raleigh now, so no doubt Viola would resume her pursuit of Daniel. At least Marie was glad that she wouldn't be in Cades Cove to observe what went on between Viola and Daniel. The talk around town about Daniel and Viola was humiliating to Marie. Could she even contemplate having anything to do with a man who had a woman staying at his house overnight? Wouldn't being seen with him tarnish her reputation?

But somehow she had a suspicion that the gossip wasn't all there was to the story. Why hadn't she let Daniel explain? Maybe she was condemning an innocent man. Oh, she would be glad to leave the Cove.

It would take only a couple of days to get the schoolhouse in order for the next fall session to start, and then after the wedding she could go home to her mother, who would understand her predicament. Her mother would be disappointed that she didn't want to continue teaching in Cades Cove the following year, but she decided to submit her resignation to the school trustees, although she hated to let them down. At least it was gratifying to know that her teaching performance had been good enough that they *wanted* her to return for the next school year.

After Viola left, Lena knocked lightly on Marie's door, and although Marie didn't want to talk, she wouldn't offend this woman who'd been so kind to her.

"Come in," she said.

Lena sat on the bed beside her and put her arm around Marie's shoulders. "My grandson is the light of my life," she said, "but he isn't perfect."

"None of us are, for that matter," Marie said between sobs. "He's really angry with me now."

"Not with you," Lena said. "He's angry at himself because he's fallen in love with you, and he's too proud to admit that he needs anyone except himself."

Lena's belief that Daniel loved her brought a bit of peace to her troubled soul, but she was still convinced that her coming to the Cove had been a mistake.

"I'm sorry I ever heard of Cades Cove. Why didn't I listen to my father and stay at home until I found somebody to marry, settle down and have a houseful of grandchildren for him to spoil?"

Lena laughed softly and kissed her on the forehead.

"Because that isn't your nature. Don't get mad at me for laughing at you, but you should know yourself well enough to realize that you're an adventuress. Consider what you've told me about your background. Your parents could have stayed in England and served the Lord there in their ministry to the unsaved in London. But, no, despite the fact that your mother was heavy with child, they set sail for the New World. After you were born, Vance Bolden would have paid your mother's fare back to England, but instead she cast her lot with a caravan of people leaving the comfort of Charleston to come by wagon train to Canaan. You and Earl were bound to inherit some of the same characteristics your parents possessed. I'm sure your mother could explain it better to you than I can. Did she object at all when you wanted to go to college and prepare to teach school?"

Grinning, Marie admitted, "No. She's a wise woman. She listened to Father quarreling about it for a few days, before she very calmly explained to him that times were changing—that women weren't necessarily destined to be only mothers and housewives in this day and age. Mother is a very clever person, and before long, I think Father thought it was his idea for me to go to college."

"Or perhaps he's as wise as your mother, and just let her *think* she was getting her way," Lena commented.

"That might be true, but they are both wonderful parents. That's why they didn't argue much when I discussed my teaching plans with them."

"There's one more thing I want to say to you tonight," Lena said, changing the subject. "Since Daniel is so stubborn he won't tell you himself, I want you to know that the night Viola went to his home and refused to leave, Daniel spent the night in the bunkhouse with his hired men. Viola was determined to snare Daniel one way or another, but after that episode, she finally gave up, realizing that he would have nothing more to do with her. Her jibes today were simply to make you jealous. She's had her eye on Daniel for a very long time, so I'm sure her pride is hurt more than anything. Do you feel better now?" Lena asked.

Sniffing, Marie said, "Thanks for telling me. I didn't mean to act like a baby and have a big crying fit."

Lena kissed her on the forehead. "Think nothing of it. Everybody needs to cry once in a while."

"The worst part is, though, I've misjudged him. In my eyes he was guilty until proven innocent. But why didn't he tell me the truth?"

"Would you have listened?" Lena asked softly.

"No," Marie admitted. "Actually, I didn't give him the chance to explain. I just believed the gossip. I owe him a big apology."

It was customary to have a picnic as a treat for the children during the last week of school. Wanting to make the children enjoy the last few days of school, and also make it memorable for them, as usual, Marie had gone to Lizzie and Lena for advice. They had proposed a picnic for Friday—the last day of school.

Lena thought the children would enjoy a hike to a log cabin a few miles from the schoolhouse, where she had taken her students on outings when she was teaching. Lizzie and Lena would accompany the group to help keep the children together and safe. Daniel was going to join them later.

On Friday morning, the sun was shining when they left the schoolhouse, and Marie commented on the good weather.

Shaking her head, Lizzie said, "I ain't so sure about that. We have to cross a mountain stream to get there, and most of the time that creek don't have much water, but I've seen it flood more than once. This time of year the weather is so unpredictable, and we could have a heavy downpour, so keep your eyes on the sky."

"Well, I'm glad you and Lena are going along and Daniel will join us later. I wouldn't know what to do if it did storm."

It was completely clear when they left the schoolhouse. The sun was shining brightly, a few fluffy clouds swirled across the blue sky and the temperature was about seventy degrees. All of the pupils had permits from their parents indicating that it was all right for their children to participate in the picnic. Lena and Marie had provided most of the food, but every child brought something to share. Even if it was no more than an apple or two, Marie accepted each contribution with pleasure.

Over the school year the older children had studied the various trees in the forest. As they walked, she asked the students to identify the different trees, and she was gratified that most of them could recognize the oaks, sycamores, maples, pines, cedars and willows. She occasionally had to caution the children to stay on the path and to walk single file. She didn't want any child to get lost, and with Lizzie walking in front and Marie bringing up the rear, they kept the children from straying off of the paths.

Everyone was ready to rest and eat lunch when they reached their destination—the ancient log cabin that was reported to have been the first cabin built in that area. Lizzie said no one knew how long ago the cabin had been built, but it looked older than any of the buildings in the Cove. Although Marie was weary from the walk, when they reached their destination, the students still had enough energy to play hide-and-seek among the trees and a few run-down outbuildings.

After they'd played several games and eaten their lunch, Marie and Lizzie decided it was time for the surprise she'd planned for them. Two people, dressed in garments of a century earlier, came out of one of the outbuildings. The children stared in surprise, and if Marie hadn't known they were coming, she would never have recognized Daniel as the man who represented John Oliver, the first permanent European settler in Cades Cove. Lena represented his wife, Lucretia Frazier. They were dressed in leather garments, like those that would have been appropriate for early settlers.

Smiling at the visitors, Marie said to the children, "Let me introduce you to John Oliver and his wife, Lucretia Frazier Oliver, who were the first settlers to settle in the Cove. Mr. Oliver, could you tell us about your first years in the Cove?"

Marie had seen Daniel in the role of businessman, grandson, neighbor and farmer, but none surpassed his acting role as the first settler to come to the Cove.

"We were poor folks," he said in the dialect of an early-century settler, "and we migrated to the Cove from the eastern seaboard. And I'm tellin' you, good people, that we'd have starved if it hadn't been for the kindness and generosity of the Cherokees. When we got to this country, all we had were a few tools and some seeds. We were totin' one youngun and had another on the way. We didn't get here in time to plant a crop, and we were a hundred miles from home, but the local natives took us in and helped us through the winter."

He continued talking about the good relationship between the Cherokee and the pioneers, ending with, "So, those of us who live here today count the Cherokee as our brothers."

So impressed was Marie by the speaking skill of Daniel that she went to him at once after the presentation was over. "Oh, thank you so much! That's the perfect ending for our school year."

Daniel put his arm around her shoulders and bent toward her. Marie's eyes widened, for she thought he intended to kiss her in front of the whole group. But the children were crowding around them, and Marie turned quickly to Lena and Lizzie and thanked them for their help, as well.

So engrossed had the children and adults been in the program and the good food that an approaching storm was the farthest thing from their minds. Suddenly a clap of thunder rolled across the treetops, and an approaching west wind found its way through the valley. Daniel jumped to his feet, horrified that he'd been so engrossed with Marie that he'd actually allowed this storm to creep up on them.

"Granny!" he shouted at the top of his voice, and Lena stepped out of the cabin. "Trouble!"

"Oh, my!" she cried when she noticed the approaching storm.

"Get all of these kids inside the cabin," Daniel shouted. "It's going to be crowded, but with the wind, the lightning and the rain, it's too dangerous for them to be outside."

Marie rushed to where a half dozen or more children were playing ball, and shouted, "Get inside the cabin right now!"

In a matter of five minutes, all of the students were accounted for, and Daniel stood in the front doorway. Lena guarded the back door to be sure none of the children sneaked out to play in the rain. There were only two small windows in the cabin, and with the near darkness outside, it wasn't a pleasant place to be.

Some time passed with the children talking excitedly about the storm, the summer vacation, the program they had just watched and various other topics of interest to them. Because this was a school function, Marie felt responsible for the welfare of everyone, and she prayed silently for God to give her the right words to encourage her pupils.

"One important fact that we all need to remember in times like these," she said, "is...who's in control of the storm? I'm your teacher, so am I the one to protect you?"

"No, ma'am," one of the older students volunteered. "God is. We learned that in Sunday School."

"That's right," Marie agreed, "so there isn't any reason for us to be afraid. God is all-powerful. Can you remember anything about floods in the Bible? If you know the answer, just go ahead and speak up without raising your hand as we do at the schoolhouse. It's too dark inside here for me to see."

"Noah sure learned about storms," one boy volunteered. "That was a long, long time ago, though. The people got so mean that God couldn't put up with 'em anymore and he wiped 'em out."

"And not only people, either," a fifth grader said. "Everything was destroyed."

"I sure hope we don't have that kind of flood today," another student said. "My Mom is making a chocolate cake for my birthday, and I don't want to miss that."

Marie was sure that she heard a muffled laugh from the corner where Daniel was standing. "Well, I wouldn't worry about missing your supper, buddy," he said, "the rain is stopping and we'll have sunlight before long."

Lena was standing next to Marie, and she whispered, "But we still might not get home for supper. These mountain streams can quickly flood and cover the trails."

Once the sun started shining, Daniel suggested that they leave right away.

"The hardest storm was on the mountain, and the high water won't get here for an hour, but it's time we headed for home. Pack up, everybody, and we'll hit the trail."

They hadn't gone very far when they encountered a surge of water in their pathway. The older children thought it was a wonderful sight to see, but the small students were scared.

One started crying, and he said, "I want my mama."

Marie looked at Daniel, and he said, "Don't cry, Buddy, you'll be with your mama tonight." Shouting, he said, "Everybody pick up your belongings and follow me. We're going to climb one little mountain and come down on the other side."

Although it took an extra hour to climb inclines to avoid the floodwater, with Daniel's guidance, Marie's encouragement and Lena and Lizzie keeping the smaller children from wading into deep water, the journey back to Cades Cove was made safely.

Chapter 8

When next morning Marie arrived at the school-house, she was both happy and sad that the school year had ended. She stabled her horse as usual, but when she started to leave the small barn, she sensed that someone was behind her. She turned quickly and screamed. A heavy hand covered her mouth and a cloth was tied over her eyes. A gag was placed over her mouth and tied behind her head. She sensed that there were two men attacking her, but they were silent. At first she'd thought that Daniel might be doing this as a joke, but she suddenly had a strong sniff of body odor, as well as the scent of tobacco, and she knew Daniel wasn't her attacker.

"Who are you? Why are you doing this?" she cried against her gag.

"Lady, if you'll do what we tell you, you ain't gonna be hurt. How much do you think your pa will pay to get your safe return?"

Another man snickered.

"And what about Daniel Watson? I hear tell that he's sweet on her. I tell you, buddy, this girl is a regular gold mine walking around on two feet. How long do you think it will take for them to cough up maybe twenty thousand dollars?"

"We'll nail one of these notices on the schoolhouse door, and put two or three others on trees in the Cove. The word will spread in a hurry."

Oh, God, she prayed silently, *what's going on?* She was lifted gently into a saddle, and she was sure she was being placed on her own horse. She sensed that one of the men rode beside her, leading Scout. Another horse followed behind.

"Lady, you won't get hurt, as long as you behave yourself," one of the men said again, gruffly, and she tried to determine if she'd ever heard his voice before. "How much money do you think you're worth to your old man? We're going to ask for ten thousand. You think he'll come up with that much money? And maybe old lady Turner might give us a little something in the meantime just to be sure we treat you right till Daddy gets here with the real money. And maybe we can get some of that gold Daniel Watson inherited."

Since she still had the gag around her mouth, Marie couldn't answer very well, and she was glad of it. What, after all, could she say? If it took every cent of their money, she had no doubt that her parents would use it to buy her freedom. And Daniel? She didn't know him well enough to make a guess as to what he might do. However, in spite of their last quarrel, which still hadn't been resolved between them, she had a feeling that Daniel would do everything he could to help her. What troubled her most was the fact that it would be several days before her parents would even learn that she'd been abducted! In the meantime, what would happen to her?

When the horses started moving, it seemed to Marie that they'd turned northwest, which would take them toward the mountains, but her sense of direction wasn't always accurate. No doubt there would be hundreds of hiding places around the Cove where she could be taken. She was scared, dreading what might happen to her, but still holding on to the faith she'd known since childhood that God was in control of her life. Always before, when she'd been faced with problems she didn't know how to solve, she'd gone to the Bible, prayed for guidance and read Scripture that encouraged her. Well, that was impossible now.

She couldn't access the Bible at the schoolhouse now, nor could she read the one in her bedroom at the Turner home. Fortunately she had memorized special passages of Scripture, and many of those came to her mind now.

"Fear thou not," God had promised in the book of Isaiah, "for I am with thee. Be not dismayed, for I am thy God: I will strengthen thee. Yea, I will help thee; yea, I will uphold thee with the right hand of My righteousness."

God, I believe that, Marie thought, and she continued to remember all of the times God had rescued His people from difficult situations.

Daniel in the lions' den.

Noah, who'd obeyed God in building an ark and trusted that he and his family would survive the largest flood ever known to humankind.

Joseph and Mary, who had obeyed God and had taken the baby Jesus to safety in Jerusalem.

Moses, who had been saved from death as a babe in Egypt and then had been chosen to lead his people into the Promised Land.

And she thought again of the fact that God had saved the life of her own mother from the raging Atlantic, which also saved the life of her and Earl. So, actually, what did she have to fear? The same God still ruled the universe today. In spite of her discomfort, her tension and her fear of death had gone.

Daniel was sorry for his last argument with Marie, but he was still angry toward her. He hadn't had a chance to talk to her privately the day before at the school picnic and hike, but he wanted to clear the air. He thought Marie's attitude toward him yesterday had softened. She didn't seem angry at him anymore and he wondered why that was. Maybe she had learned the truth about Viola. He sure hoped so because she hadn't been willing to listen to him.

He had considered returning to the schoolhouse

and apologizing after their argument, but had decided it was better for him to delay his apology. If there was any future for them together, she would have to learn eventually that he wasn't a man who would let a woman boss him around. Although he had to admit that Marie really didn't come across as a female who intended to have her way, come what may, but he didn't want her to think that he was a man who could be led around like a pet dog, either. He had returned to his farm, and helped his two farmhands do the evening chores.

After mulling it over, he had cooled off. He knew she'd be at the schoolhouse today cleaning, and he again considered going over and apologizing. He did the morning chores alongside his farm hands, then headed for the house for lunch. He heard the phone ringing the minute he stepped inside the house. He figured it was his grandmother calling because there weren't many people who ever tried to contact him by telephone. When he took the receiver off the wall and held it to his ear, his grandmother's voice said, "Is Marie with you?"

The words and the terror in her voice caused him to gasp. "Why, no, I haven't seen her since yesterday. When was she supposed to come home?"

"She was going to the school for a few hours to start getting ready for next year, but she said she'd be home by noon. She's an hour late, and that's not like her. I called Lizzie Crossen and asked her to see if Marie's horse was still in the stable. It isn't, but there's a note on the schoolhouse door that struck terror into my heart like I've never known before. It's addressed to me and you."

"Well," he said impatiently, "what's in the note?"

"How much do you think Vance Bolden will pay to get his daughter back with nary a hair on her head touched? Ten thousand, maybe. Ever day that goes by the ransom mite get a lot bigger. And what Vance hands out, you can make up yore mind to match it."

Lena's voice was strained, as she said, "I'm afraid, Daniel. We can raise the money, but I don't know how soon we can get in touch with the Boldens. And I'm sure Marie is really frightened at what might happen to her in the meantime."

"I'll kill any man who lays a hand on her."

"Oh, Daniel, don't say such a thing! I'm going to start praying that she'll be brought back to us unharmed."

For the first time since he'd fought in the recent war, Daniel was frightened. He could always make up his mind at a minute's notice, but now he was at a loss to know what to do. When he hung up the phone receiver, he dropped to his knees, his body shaking all over.

"God, it's been so long since I've even given You any thought, to say nothing of calling on You. I'm ashamed, but don't punish Marie for my shortcomings. What can I do? Where could she be?"

Daniel knew he desperately needed some help, but

he was hesitant to leave the area in case there were more messages to indicate Marie's whereabouts. Choosing a young Cherokee, Bralin, which meant mighty warrior, who was working on his farm, he said, "Do you know where Earl Bolden lives?"

The Cherokee nodded. "I do. Awinta is my sister."

He quickly explained about Marie's abduction.

"Not only do I want to get a message to Earl, I want you to have Earl find Mitali and Deerfoot, the best trackers in the Cherokee nation, and bring them back here. If anyone can find Marie, they can. When will you leave?"

"Soon as I go to the bunkhouse and change into my buckskins. I never go to the reservation without looking like a native."

"I'm going with you," Daniel said.

Bralin gave Daniel a skeptical look and shook his head. "You'd better stay here, in case other messages come. Besides, it's every man for himself on a hunt like this, and when those trackers get started, it's not easy to keep up."

Daniel shook his head. "I'll keep up. I'll go crazy if I just wait here doing nothing. And while we're waiting on them, I want to go to the schoolhouse and see if there are any clues we might have missed."

"I'll go with you," the Cherokee said. "But first I'll send someone to find Earl and the trackers."

Although the two men searched the area around the schoolhouse from one end to the other, they couldn't detect anything that pointed to Marie's abduction.

"Too many kids' tracks, as well as the hooves of horses," Bralin said. "We'll have to wait till morning."

By the time the two scouts and Earl arrived the next morning, Daniel had gathered all the weapons they could carry easily, along with enough food to keep an army for days. Thus supplied, the group headed for the mountains. The next three days were the most miserable hours that Daniel had ever spent. Not only did climbing the mountains and keeping up with the three agile Cherokees test his physical endurance to the limit, he was so concerned about what might be happening to Marie that he was frantic. Mentally he came up with all kinds of possible scenarios that she might be enduring until he thought he would lose his mind. He ate food, not because he was hungry, but because he wanted to be physically able to keep up with the others.

Late in the evening of the third day of their searching, Deerfoot held up a cautioning hand when they topped another hilltop and looked into a rocky ravine. Imperiously, he motioned to his companions to follow his example and drop to the ground.

"I just saw two men come out of a cave across that ravine," Deerfoot said. "They're probably holding Marie a captive in that cave. They had their bow and arrows, so I figure they're going to look for food before nightfall, but wouldn't use their guns for they don't want to alert anybody to their whereabouts. I'll go down and investigate the cave, and if Marie is there, I'll bring her out. If the men come back before I bring her to safety, shoot to warn them away."

Daniel nodded acceptance, as did Earl. Although Daniel chafed at the inactivity, he realized that the Cherokee would be more help to Marie at this point than they would be. Daniel took his watch from his pocket and monitored the time as Deerfoot walked cautiously down the rugged terrain. Every minute seemed like an hour to him, and he knew without a doubt that he loved Marie. For the first time in his life, he'd found a woman he wanted to marry. But could he ever live up to the standards that Marie expected in a husband? Although he loved his grandmother devotedly, he'd always thought she was too strict in her religious beliefs. For a moment he considered bargaining with God.

If You'll bring Marie back safely to me, then I'll mend my ways and follow You!

No, that wouldn't do. From his childhood when he'd attended Sunday school, he remembered that one of his teachers had said, "You can't bargain with God."

He had gone further to explain, "Just keep in mind what the Scriptures say. 'He that knoweth to do good and doeth it not, to him it is sin.'"

Many times since then, Daniel had tried to forget that admonition, but at the most unexpected times, it popped into his mind.

Was he, Daniel Watson, man enough to admit that he wasn't perfect and take upon himself the yoke of servitude that was expected of those who served God? He didn't know.

So quietly did the Cherokees move that Daniel didn't even know Deerfoot had returned until he touched Daniel on the shoulder. He was so tense that he jumped like a rabbit, and Deerfoot said, "Sorry, I didn't mean to frighten you."

"What did you find?"

"Nothing except this." He took a white silk scarf from his pocket. "Could it belong to Miss Bolden?"

"I think I've seen her wear that scarf, or one like it, but I'm not sure."

Cautioning Daniel to walk carefully and keep his eyes peeled in case one of the kidnappers should be stalking them, the Cherokees started descending the mountain path. "She's probably in that cave right below us. Walk carefully and watch for anything and everything. No talking," Mitali said.

Although Daniel thought the walk would never end, it wasn't more than a half hour when they reached the level spot in front of the cave.

Mitali held up a hand for silence and motioned for Daniel to come to his side. "Since your friend doesn't know us, it might be well for you to go into the cave and let her know we're here. She'll probably be tied, or the men wouldn't have left her alone."

"And it's possible that there might be more than two kidnappers—with one in the cave watching her, so be cautious," Bralin warned.

When they reached the mouth of the cave, using a piece of flint, Mitali started a flame on a cedar branch. "This isn't a deep cave," he said, "so she'll be close to the door. I'll follow you and hold the light. God go with you!"

Daniel nodded, and his pulse accelerated until he was breathless as he stepped into the cave and paused until his eyes adjusted to the dim light.

"Marie," he whispered, "are you in here?"

He listened carefully, and when she didn't answer, Mitali moved closer to Daniel, and he said, "Maybe this isn't the right cave."

Daniel flashed the light around the cave. It was a small area, and one glance proved that Marie was no longer in the cave.

"So what do we do now?"

"Wait for daylight, and then we hit the trail."

"I can't stand to think of her being alone with them tonight."

"I've prayed that God will protect her through the night," Mitali said. "I believe God answered the prayer. We'll go back to the Cove, pack anything we need and hit the trail as soon as daylight comes."

"Can't we look around a little more now? I spent a lot of time climbing these mountains when I was a boy, and there's more than one cave on this mountain."

Daniel sensed that the Cherokee thought it was a waste of time, but he nodded agreement, and Daniel picked up a lantern and they moved forward cautiously. The terrain was rugged, and progress was slow; when the eastern sky lightened with the rising of the sun, Daniel said, "You were right, of course.

We need to be more men than this. Let's return to Cades Cove and organize a larger party."

Disillusioned, as well as frightened, Daniel walked dejectedly down the trail. A sound distracted him. He looked into a small cave and saw Marie writhing on the ground in front of him. Her hands and feet were tied and a gag was in her mouth. So angry at her attackers for treating her that way that he almost choked, Daniel dropped to his knees beside her and pulled the gag over her head.

He put his arm around her waist and helped her stand, then untied her hands. Holding her close, he whispered, "Have they harmed you?"

"Oh, no," she said weakly. "No, they left almost as soon as they brought me here, but they've checked on me a few times. Oh, Daniel, I've been so scared."

"So have I," he said. "I love you so much I couldn't bear the thought that they might have assaulted you."

Sobbing, Marie said, "Oh, nothing like that, but the gag hurt my mouth, and my hands are tied so tight that they're numb. I've been miserable."

Bralin, carrying a pine torch, entered the cave and Marie clung to Daniel.

"Who is it?" she cried, fear in her voice.

"Friends, my dear. Cherokee friends of Earl's and mine. If it hadn't been for them, we might not have found you."

Later, warm, safe and well fed at Lena's house, Marie talked over her long ordeal with her parents and friends. She had been frightened and uncomfortable, but her faith had kept her going through her trial, and she realized she was braver and stronger than she ever imagined.

After everyone had heard the entire story, Earl related how he and the Cherokee had waited for the perpetrators and caught them going back to the cave shortly after Marie was rescued.

Vance said, "I'm glad you're coming home, Marie, where I can look after you."

"Oh, Dad. Bad things can happen anywhere."

"Well," her father replied, "you were never kidnapped in Canaan. I don't think you're safe here, an unmarried woman alone in that schoolhouse."

Daniel said, "Mr. Bolden, the kidnappers were just a couple of hoodlums from Chestnut Flats looking for a quick way to make a lot of money. Fortunately they weren't very smart and didn't plan very well. They didn't have any ill will toward Marie and they didn't try to hurt her. They just wanted money."

"Still," Vance said, "they scared three years off my life and I am glad my daughter is going home with her mother and me."

Daniel took Marie's hand and led her to the front porch, leaving everyone else to discuss the matter. They sat down in the rockers and Daniel said, "Marie, I'm sorry about our last argument. We never resolved it and I've felt terrible that we didn't clear the air. I don't like it when we're mad at each other."

Marie smiled and said, "I don't like it, either. Daniel, Lena told me what really happened with Viola the night she stayed at your house. I'm sorry I didn't listen when you tried to explain. I'm even sorrier that I listened to gossip. I know better. It's just that Viola is so infuriating."

"Then you won't be surprised to hear that she was the source of the gossip. Some people have no shame."

"Wasn't she concerned about tarnishing her own reputation?"

"Viola plans to leave here. She probably doesn't care what people think."

Daniel scooted his chair closer to Marie's and took her hand. "Let's not talk about Viola. She's already in the past. Besides, we have other things to discuss."

Chapter 9

Marie eagerly awaited Earl and Awinta's wedding because she had never attended a Cherokee ceremony. When Awinta and Earl arrived for the wedding, Marie thought she'd never seen a more beautiful bride. The dress she wore was a family heirloom—a dress made from the skin of an albino deer, which had also been worn by Awinta's mother and grandmother on their respective wedding days. Although Earl generally wore buckskin garments year round, in deference to the feelings of his parents, he wore a dark blue knee-length coat with check-tweed trousers, a single-breasted waistcoat, a stiff shirt with studs and a small white bow tie.

Marie wore a dress her mother had ordered from Charleston especially for the occasion. Her garment was made of dark blue cloth trimmed with bands of gold embroidery on the bodice and sleeves. She wore a matching velvet hat trimmed with a feather and a blue ribbon.

The traditional Cherokee wedding ritual took place first in the churchyard before a group of Cherokee and a large crowd of Cades Cove residents. The pastor, who was broadminded, had been willing for the Cherokee spiritual leader to use the church sanctuary, although the leader politely refused, saying that it was not traditional for the wedding service to take place in a building.

The bride was represented by both her mother and brother. Awinta's oldest brother, Atohi, stood beside them as Earl vowed to accept the responsibility of teaching any children they had in spiritual and religious matters.

Marie was pleasantly surprised when the ceremony turned out to be such a solemn and meaningful occasion. To start the festivities, the couple drank together from a Cherokee wedding vase that had been used by the bride's family for years. The vase was filled with tart grape juice, and it had two openings for the couple to drink from at the same time.

Instead of exchanging rings, the bride and groom exchanged food. Earl brought a ham of deer meat, as an indication that he would provide for his household. Awinta provided several ears of corn and some bean bread as a sign that she would provide nourishment for her household. These traditional gifts indicated that the groom was associated with hunting and providing, while the bride's offering showed her intention of giving life and nourishment to her family.

The sacred spot for the ceremony had been blessed for seven consecutive days before the ceremony started. Awinta and Earl approached the sacred fire and were blessed by the tribal priest. Traditional songs were sung in Cherokee before the bride and groom were covered in a blue blanket at the beginning of the vows. At the close of the ceremony, they were wrapped in a white blanket, indicating the beginning of a new life together.

After the Cherokee wedding was celebrated on the lawn, the pastor of the church invited the assembled group to enter the church to witness the Christian wedding of Earl and Awinta. The pews were filled; there was standing room only.

The structure was fairly new, having replaced the original dirt-floored log cabin a few years after the first building had been destroyed by fire. The sanctuary had two front doors, for the purpose of having men enter the church and sit on one side of the sanctuary, with women and children on the other side. A wide aisle down the middle of the church separated the two. It had been several years since this practice had been enforced, and men and their families usually sat together in one pew.

Marie was surprised at the large group of people who'd gathered for the wedding, but Lena whispered, "Awinta's family are leaders of the Cherokees, and I expected a large crowd. I didn't know that they would all stay for the traditional wedding inside the church, but I'm happy they did."

In deference to those who couldn't understand the Cherokee language, Earl had asked the local preacher to read in English two selections of poetry that were always a part of the Cherokee wedding.

Marie considered it an inspiring addition to the service, as was the preacher's Cherokee blessing, which he pronounced on the young couple.

A male soloist, who sang in the Christian church on the Cherokee reservation, sang "The Indian Serenade," first in Cherokee and then in English.

As Earl and Awinta stood before the minister, he asked Daniel and Marie to take their places as attendants on each side of the couple. When the minister started reading the traditional wedding service, "Dearly beloved, we are gathered together here in the sight of God and these witnesses..." Daniel lifted his hand.

"Could we pause for a moment?"

Reverend Thomas had been in the ministry for many years and apparently he was never surprised at what might happen in any service.

"Of course," he answered with a smile, "what's on your mind?"

Daniel opened his mouth, and Marie had never before seen him so flustered. His face had turned beet red, and he cleared his throat several times before he finally mumbled, "Well, I've just realized how much I love Marie. If she's willing, why can't you marry us, too?"

Still smiling, the minister said quietly, "You certainly don't mean right now?"

"Yes, I do."

Daniel turned to Marie, put his arm around her shoulders and pulled her close.

Speaking to her as if they were the only people in the sanctuary, he said, "I know this is most irregular, but since we've known one another for several months, by now, you're probably not surprised at anything I do. Regardless of how you answer my question, I doubt I'll change much. Will you marry me?"

"Yes, of course..." she started to say, and when he opened his lips to speak, she shook her head. "Please let me finish. I *want* to marry you, but don't you think you'd better get permission from someone else?"

He stared at her, not comprehending.

"Oh, you mean your parents!" Daniel said, and groaned aloud. "What if they say no?" he whispered.

Marie shrugged her shoulders, enjoying herself immensely. It was good to realize that her future husband *could be* uncertain about what he said or did.

Taking a deep breath, he turned toward the seat where Vance and Evelyn sat.

"Will you give us your blessing for this marriage?"

"Certainly," Vance said, "I believe the two of you *deserve one another,* and I'll leave it up to you to interpret what I mean by that answer."

After a moment of stunned silence, the congregation burst into spontaneous laughter and applause at Vance's answer.

"Certainly you aren't suggesting that they have the wedding right now?" Evelyn said to Vance. "I only have one daughter, and I want to see her married in our own church in Canaan. That is, if it's acceptable to Daniel's grandmother."

She turned to Lena. "Since you're Daniel's closest relative, what's your idea about planning a wedding?"

"I wholeheartedly approve of Marie marrying into our family. I, too, want to see them marry in a church wedding, and I approve Canaan as the place for it."

Shamefaced, Daniel said, "Forget my hasty proposal. I agree that we should postpone our wedding for a few weeks until you ladies can make plans for a day that we'll all remember with pride and pleasure." He turned to the minister and said, "Forgive me for interrupting the wedding. Please go on."

The minister laughed as if he'd seen everything, then continued with Earl and Awinta's wedding.

Although Daniel would have been willing for the minister in Cades Cove to perform the wedding at the same time as Earl and Awinta's, he could understand why Evelyn, Lena and Marie wanted a formal ceremony. As they talked about it later back at his grandmother's house, he said, "I'll admit that I didn't consider that you ladies would want to make our wedding such a big event. Buy anything and everything you want to, and I'll pay for it."

Shaking her head, Evelyn smiled and said, "I doubt that your future father-in-law will allow that. The bride's parents are traditionally responsible for the wedding expenses. Although Vance will probably tell us that you should have a simple wedding like ours was, he wouldn't consider allowing you to pay the bill."

"What kind of wedding ceremony did you have?" Daniel wanted to know, realizing that he'd attended only a few weddings in his lifetime.

"We stood on the steps of the Bolden plantation home and had a very simple service. The plantation employees and close neighbors attended, and I wore garments that we found in the trunks of Bolden ancestors, stored in the attic. I still have those clothes and, while they are treasures to keep, I think Marie should have a new dress."

Shrugging his shoulders, Daniel said, "She'll be beautiful no matter what she wears, and if Vance wants to pay the bills, that's all right with me."

Marie turned to Daniel and took his hand. "After the wedding could we go to South Carolina where Daddy's plantation was, and visit the island where Earl and I were born? We could include it in our honeymoon."

Daniel said, "I reserve the right to take you on a wedding trip, and I'd like to go to New York, if that appeals to you."

Smiling broadly, Marie agreed. "More than all right! I've always wanted to go to New York. We can go to South Carolina later."

Daniel nodded and said, "We haven't discussed it, but after our honeymoon I'd like us to settle down in my house in the Cove. Is that all right with you?"

"I love you so much I'll agree to anything you want to do," she said, taking both his hands and gazing into his eyes.

Content to let Lena and Evelyn plan the wedding, Marie readily accepted when Lena asked if she could make the wedding gown. Marie was pleased that the styles for women's garments were changing. No longer did the styles favor crinolines and bustles, but rather the skirts in front were cut slim at the top and flared at the bottom. Two pleats were located in the back, where a bustle would have been placed a few years earlier. She also intended to wear a gold bouquet holder, a gift from her father, as well as the watch attached to an ornamental brooch that Vance had given to Evelyn on the occasion of their tenth wedding anniversary.

With all the plans to be made, the time passed quickly until the day she stood before the altar of the church in Canaan, dressed in a white satin dress and wearing a matching wide-brimmed hat. Beside her, Daniel stood, handsome as always, outfitted in a dark brown double-breasted morning coat, matching trousers, and a white shirt with a wing collar. The church was crowded with family and friends, and as they took their vows, Marie recalled the events of her life. It seemed that she'd come full circle from the time she was born to this time of rejoicing with friends and relatives on this special day.

Only a short distance from the church was the place where she'd seen Daniel for the first time—riding a bucking bronco. Her life hadn't been the same since then. Momentarily, she wondered what God had in the future for them. Perhaps it was as well she didn't know. Still, Marie was sure that, in spite of several traumatic situations, because God had brought her this far, He would continue to guide her decisions. They returned to the Bolden mansion where Aunt Fannie and her helpers had prepared enough food to feed a small army.

As they walked up the front steps, suddenly a bright ray of sunshine escaped from a white cloud that was flitting across the sky and spotlighted the steps of the Bolden mansion where they were standing.

"I consider that a good sign—God is putting His blessing on us," Marie said. "Our relationship hasn't been altogether perfect so far, but as we've walked our individual ways, now we'll walk hand in hand together. Oh, Daniel, God *is* good."

"Yes, He is," Daniel agreed. "I'm so thankful that I'm following Him now, so we'll have a Christian home where we will be blessed and have the opportunity to watch our children grow to adulthood. I'm looking forward to that journey."

Moving into his tight embrace, Marie whispered, "So am I, Daniel. So am I!"

Momentarily, Marie's past flitted through her

mind. It had been quite a journey, and not one she would want to repeat. But the future beckoned to her, so she accepted the challenge. Whatever God had in mind for Daniel and her, she would gladly accept.

Epilogue

After their month-long trip to New York City, Marie thought that she would be satisfied to settle down in Cades Cove the rest of her life. When she commented on this to her mother, Evelyn laughed.

"You? I'm not too sure about that! Earl, yes. But you'll always want to see what's on the other side of the mountain. Isn't there some place in particular you'd like to visit before you settle down and, I hope, plan to provide me with some grandchildren?"

"Oh, don't put ideas in her head," Daniel said. "I have a farm to manage."

Grinning sheepishly, Marie said, "Someday I want to go to California, but not until we have those grandchildren you've mentioned."

Daniel groaned, but she ignored him because she knew he wanted to visit the West Coast, too.

"But in the meantime," she said, turning to Daniel, "there's a place I want to visit more than California, and I want to take Dad and Mother with us."

"Name it, and we'll all go," Daniel said.

Silently amused, Marie wondered if she told Daniel she wanted the moon if he would try to get it for her.

"I want to visit Charleston and see those places that molded my life. I'd especially like to see the island where Dad rescued my mother, and where Earl and I were born." She turned to her mother and said, "Do you think Dad would want to go?"

"We'll never know until we ask."

When Marie questioned her father about the trip to the Atlantic coast, he agreed that he would like to visit the former Bolden Plantation.

"I sort of dread it," Vance said, "for it might be run down, and I'll always remember the mansion like it is now, rather than what it was when I was a child."

"I'm looking forward to seeing our ancestral home and I wish Earl could go with us, but that isn't an option," Marie said. "He said he really didn't want to go."

Daniel laughed, saying, "If you and Earl didn't look so much alike, I wouldn't believe you were even related. Earl is a quiet, rather reclusive person, with hardly any interest in other people. Or so it seems."

"Yes, we are different. But he's been a good brother. He's always been attentive to me. When we were children, we were inseparable. He was my protector, too, and made it a point to see that no one pestered me. It's true he's not as outgoing as I am, though."

A month later, when they arrived at the plantation where he was born, tears momentarily filled Vance's eyes. Marie took his hand. "Are you disappointed, Daddy?"

"Oh, no! I dreaded to see it, but the property looks exactly as it did when I first remember it. The ravages of war are gone now, and I can remember how my sister and I played as children on the lawn." Pointing to a hill behind the house, he continued, "Our family cemetery is up there. I hope the owners will give us permission to visit it."

Not only did the current owners tell them they could go to the cemetery, they also took them on a tour of the house. When they left, Evelyn said quietly to the owner, "Thank you so much for your hospitality. In the past few years, my husband has wondered if his ancestral home was in good hands. It's a blessing to both of us that his memories of the plantation are pleasant."

The next day, they hired a buggy and took a tour of the town, stopping along the coast to see the island where the twins were born. Only a pile of logs was left of the cabin where Vance had cared for Evelyn during the birth of the twins.

"Well, Father, Mother, you've come full circle

since 1875." Marie asked, "Looking back, do you have regrets, sorrows, joy?"

Vance's eyes were full of tears, and he couldn't speak. He nodded toward Evelyn, and putting her arm around him, she beckoned for Daniel and Marie to join them. With their arms intertwined, she said, "I've experienced some of all those emotions. But ours has been a full life, and my prayer is that your marriage will be as rewarding as ours has been. I'm suddenly reminded of some words from the 126th Psalm, which, to my notion, describe our lives in detail. I couldn't ask for a better promise than these words, 'The Lord hath done great things for us; whereof we are glad... He that goeth forth and weepeth, bearing precious seed, shall doubtless come again with rejoicing, bringing his sheaves with him.'"

"I know it's impossible," Marie said, "but I sometimes wish we could see into the future and know what the next twenty years will bring. Still, we do have the assurance that God is faithful and will guide our future as He has our past. God is good!"

Vance, Daniel and Evelyn agreed to her words with a resounding, "Amen!"

* * * * *

REQUEST YOUR FREE BOOKS!

2 FREE CHRISTIAN NOVELS
PLUS 2
FREE
MYSTERY GIFTS

HEARTSONG
PRESENTS

YES! Please send me 2 Free Heartsong Presents novels and my 2 FREE mystery gifts (gifts are worth about $10). After receiving them, if I don't wish to receive any more books I can return the shipping statement marked "cancel." If I don't cancel, I will receive 4 brand-new novels every month and be billed just $4.24 per book in the U.S. and $5.24 per book in Canada. That's a savings of at least 20% off the cover price. It's quite a bargain! Shipping and handling is just 50¢ per book in the U.S. and 75¢ per book in Canada.* I understand that accepting the 2 free books and gifts places me under no obligation to buy anything. I can always return a shipment and cancel at any time. Even if I never buy another book, the two free books and gifts are mine to keep forever.

159/359 HDN FVYK

Name	(PLEASE PRINT)
Address	Apt. #
City	State	Zip

Signature (if under 18, a parent or guardian must sign)

Mail to the Harlequin® Reader Service:
IN U.S.A.: P.O. Box 1867, Buffalo, NY 14240-1867

* Terms and prices subject to change without notice. Prices do not include applicable taxes. Sales tax applicable in N.Y. This offer is limited to one order per household. Not valid for current subscribers to Heartsong Presents books. All orders subject to credit approval. Credit or debit balances in a customer's account(s) may be offset by any other outstanding balance owed by or to the customer. Please allow 4 to 6 weeks for delivery. Offer available while quantities last. Offer valid only in the U.S.

Your Privacy—The Harlequin® Reader Service is committed to protecting your privacy. Our Privacy Policy is available online at www.ReaderService.com or upon request from the Harlequin Reader Service.
We make a portion of our mailing list available to reputable third parties that offer products we believe may interest you. If you prefer that we not exchange your name with third parties, or if you wish to clarify or modify your communication preferences, please visit us at www.ReaderService.com/consumerschoice or write to us at Harlequin Reader Service Preference Service, P.O. Box 9062, Buffalo, NY 14269. Include your complete name and address.

HSPDIR13R

HEARTSONG
PRESENTS

Look out for 4 new
Heartsong Presents books next month!

**Every month 4 inspiring faith-filled
romances will be available in stores.**

These contemporary and historical Christian
romances emphasize God's role in every
relationship and reinforce the importance of
faith, hope and love.